Selected Short Stories

by Ludmil Todorov

Printed in the United States of America

Accents Publishing
Editor: Bissera Kostova
Cover Design by Kiril Zlatkov
Typesetting by Asen Iliev
Translated from the Bulgarian by Zlatna Kostova and Matey Todorov

Library of Congress Control Number: 2021942084
ISBN: 978-1-936628-82-7

First Edition

SELECTED SHORT STORIES

by LUDMIL TODOROV

Translated from the Bulgarian
by ZLATNA KOSTOVA and MATEY TODOROV

Contents

AN INSOLENT BON VIVANT

Evgeni Sabev slept at most four hours a night, and quite reluctantly. He went to bed at one in the morning and got up at five with such zeal that his family had to put earplugs in their ears. First, Evgeni would go into the bathroom, then feed the two dogs, fry bacon and eggs for himself, make coffee in a noisy coffee machine, and do the dishes left from the night before. This was a crucial moment for the sleep of his wife and their two daughters, because, no matter how careful Evgeni was, the clinking of a plate at five in the morning can wake a whole building, let alone three jumpy women with plugged ears, who are only waiting to be awoken and – just like fairies in white gowns – to rush to Evgeni and demand an explanation: why.

"Why, Dad, why are you doing the dishes at five in the morning?"

"You could have done them last night."

"The dishes were done by me last night, but then you obviously ate again."

"Just a bite."

"Did you cook?"

"Never mind."

Between six and seven in the morning Evgeni Sabev walked the two dogs. Then, he would take another shower, this time singing. At about seven-thirty he usually started craving human company, so he'd pester one of the three – whoever was unlucky enough to get up first – by greeting her good morning with a Russian folk verse or deliver a lecture on a global problem like the fate of the polar bears, or the imminent demise of the Amazon rainforest.

Evgeni Sabev had studied library science and was a man of vast knowledge and many interests. He recited equally well poems by Penyu Penev, Yesenin, Eliot, and Whitman; sang songs by Elton John, accompanied by details of Elton and David's same sex marriage and their two adopted children. The crisis in Bulgaria at the end of the last century forced Evgeni to abandon his true vocation to be a librarian and a scholar, and go into the mortuary business.

In the early 90's he had two prospects before him: to go into the butchery and cured meats business, or the business of burying the deceased. Evgeni chose the latter, partly because he sensed that sooner or later the big sharks would throw him out of the meat business, partly because despite his great love of meat and meat products, burying people appealed to him more. He was a gourmet and loved to indulge himself, but not at all costs. His choice of study to be a librarian was indicative: the humanities of all varieties captivated him more than a juicy steak, believe it or not.

Sabev's younger daughter was a student of psychology, and the elder one had a degree in Bulgarian philology. They both worked at their father's funeral home. Their mother did the book-keeping. The Sabevs' funeral agency had three offices: two in the suburbs and one downtown.

Sabev's three beloved women were dark-eyed, jet-haired, beautiful, and prone to melancholy. They hated the family business. It was not an easy field and all three of them had tried to quit. When Sabev first suggested that his wife become an accountant at his funeral home, she, having been trained in community service, laughed at him. For two years she struggled as the director of a community center, then she certified as an accountant and took on the book-keeping of the agency.

The elder daughter was ashamed to say what exactly her parents' business was. Sabev's wife came up with a formulation that everyone began using when needed: they were in the rituals business.

The younger daughter took her family's occupation in stride, and applied to study psychology at the university, in order to learn how to deal with people, who had suffered a great loss. She soon realized that her academic knowledge had no practical application and got depressed. She sulked, and was always on the verge of tears, while her father did his best to comfort her:

"Where do you want me to send you to school? Do you want to go to London? I'll send you to London to study something else!"

Evgeni Sabev had granted his beautiful, jet-haired, nervous women freedom of choice, but in the end they all came back to the funeral home. The two daughters ran the suburban offices, he managed the downtown office, while the mother did the book-keeping from home. Besides them, he had also employed a hearse driver, two assistants to his daughters, an assistant for himself, a make-up artist, and two women to bathe the deceased. Evgeni often entertained the staff at his home, and occasionally took them out to a restaurant. His daughters hated these gatherings. When he threw the parties at home, Evgeni wouldn't stop singing, and when they went out to a restaurant, he'd order a huge amount of spicy meatballs, which he ate by himself with such evident delight, one would think he was putting up a show.

To evade his annoying merriment, his daughters often went to symphony concerts. He would ask them what they had listened to and then, for the rest of the evening, he'd hum pieces from the symphonies mentioned.

Evgeni Sabev was a true nightmare for his loved ones, but when he stopped being like that, they'd immediately get worried.

"What's the matter, Dad?" they would ask, when Sabev happened to stop making noise for more than ten seconds.

Evgeni rarely stopped making noise for more than ten seconds. Even when he wasn't talking, he grunted, snorted, whistled, giggled and when he made none of these, he just breathed. Sometimes his breathing was more eloquent than words. Evgeni Sabev weighed over a hundred kilos and breathed like a man who weighs over a hundred kilos. If he stopped breathing that way, everyone, the two dogs included, would give him a questioning glance. At such moments, Evgeni usually came up with ideas related to the advertising activity of the funeral home or the quality of the food in plastic containers they prepared for the mourners. Even his fastidious relatives found this food delicious.

The Sabevs' agency offered several menus. The most modest one included boiled wheat, home-made bread, pretzels and pastries. A certain shop cooked the traditional boiled wheat, another one made the bread, yet another made the pretzels, and a fourth made the pastries, instead of having everything prepared in one place, which turned out to be impossible, because the shop whose boiled wheat was good, made soggy bread, and the bakery with the delicious pretzels failed in the pastries department. Just to fill a plastic plate with edible food, Evgeni Sabev had been taking pains for several years.

People hardly realize how important it is for mourners to be offered good food at a funeral. If the pretzels you eat stick to the palate and leave a rancid taste, this taste also sticks to your memories of the deceased. Moreover, death itself begins to taste rancid, instead of tasting like fresh home-made bread. Evgeni

Sabev used to regularly inspect each item on the menu. At a first foul up he'd give the caterer a warning; at the second one, he'd replace him. All of this was only a small part of his duties as head of the funeral home.

Evgeni's two daughters were perfect for the job they were doing, namely, making first contact with the relatives of the deceased. Their innate melancholy created an atmosphere that other funeral homes worked hard to achieve. The two girls radiated deep sadness, even at the sight of a run in their stockings.

Evgeni Sabev opened the downtown office to serve a better-off clientele. He once buried the relative of a mobster. The mobster ordered a wood-carved oak coffin that cost 4,500 leva. Shortly after the funeral service, the coffin with the body of the deceased was cremated. There were also reputable rich people, who didn't hold back on what they'd spend on their deceased. Thus, with half the number of funerals, the central office began to make the same profit as the suburban offices.

One evening the death of a great Bulgarian poet was announced on TV. On the following day, two men came to the central office to arrange the poet's funeral. The younger one was a representative of the Ministry of Culture. Evgeni was moved at the opportunity to personally manage the burial of one of his favorite poets, and expressed his grief. This seemed to annoy the older man:

"Let's get to the point," he growled.

"Favorite poet, my foot, you despicable saleseman!" that's what this extremely disagreeable person wanted to say.

Evgeni felt deeply offended and to prove the sincerity of his words he was about to start reciting one of the dead poet's famous poems, but then decided not to, and his face acquired a sleepy expression.

　　　　

The Ministry official buried himself in a folder. In the silence, all that was heard was Evgeni's breathing.

"Well, let's begin," said the Ministry official.

What followed was so embarrassing that Evgeni, who was merely taking notes of what was expected from him, blushed. The Ministry official announced that he had a limited budget, and he and the unpleasant man, who turned out to be a literary critic and friend of the deceased, began haggling over the choice of coffin, wreath, menu and all the small accessories related to the ceremony.

The two men went through the catalogs Evgeni offered them, arguing whether the coffin should be made of plywood at a price of two hundred, or solid wood for fifteen hundred; whether the wreath should be made from two kinds of flowers for seventy leva, or six kinds of flowers for two hundred and fifty; whether to include cheese and rice-stuffed vine leaves in the menu or not; what the red wine should be. The literary critic insisted that the wine be from the late poet's favorite brand, and the Ministry official said it was too expensive.

This was normal practice at Evgeni's office. Every client cuts their coat according to their cloth. In this case, however, it was a great Bulgarian poet they were going to bury, and Evgeni refused to believe that a whole ministry was stingy with such things. He wondered if the late poet's relatives were so flat broke as to leave it to the State to cover all the costs.

Still, in the dispute between the two men, Evgeni sided with the Ministry guy who had a limited budget and there was very little he could do. His nasty opponent attacked him with such sarcasm, as if expecting the man to produce the money out of his own pocket. *Why don't you pay for it, then!* Evgeni thought, hidden behind his computer.

Evgeni could not deny the critic's polemic fervor, used to defend a just cause, and secretly admired his rich vocabulary and skill at making a laughing stock out of his opponent. The dispute soon went beyond the scope of coffins, wreaths, wine and wheat and extended to the spiritual values of the country. The critic said it was humiliating for him to bargain over a bowl of boiled wheat and he warned he'd enlighten the public regarding the monstrous choice of a plywood coffin in which the glory of Bulgaria would rest. Having made these fancy accusations, he left the funeral home. The Ministry official, who was not impressed by his words in the least, confirmed the order for a plywood coffin.

In the evening, Evgeni Sabev came home agitated and began telling his family what had happened. For the first time since his career had taken this bizarre direction, he realized that not all people die. Some continue to live after their death, and Evgeni had the rare privilege to bury one of them. He felt not only at the center of events in his country, but also at the center of life itself. His excitement was so strong that the dogs couldn't bear it and started barking at him fiercely. Evgeni was outraged at the way society was set to bid farewell to a great poet and the three women had to listen to him going on and on:

"Incredible!... Unbelievable!... Incredible and unbelievable!"

In the next couple of days, Sabev devoted all his time to this funeral. At his own expense, he bought the late poet's favorite wine. He ordered a solid wood coffin for fifteen hundred leva. In the carpenter's shop they gave him a 50% discount and even offered to carve the coffin for free, but he turned down the offer. He told them to make the coffin plain. Then, he personally selected the flowers for the wreath and asked the florist to make it a most extraordinary wreath, and not the cheap bunch of flowers that was ordered. He also paid special attention to the food:

to the usual menu he added some delicious stuffed vine leaves, not canned, but made by a caterer he knew well. He also added a few slices of scrumptious cured pork loin, as well as a piece of white cheese. He ordered that the wine and soft drinks be served in glasses, not in the usual plastic cups.

On the day of the funeral, he put on his best mourning suit and went to supervise the dressing and makeup application of the deceased. Many people frowned at the idea of makeup. The funeral homes would explain that their makeup application is subtle, almost imperceptible, with the sole purpose of making the deceased look well, but most people apparently imagined a painted Egyptian mummy and would refuse make-up.

After the deceased was dressed and made up under Evgeni's personal supervision, Evgeni asked his assistant to accompany the hearse and went to the central church, where the service was going to be held. Before that, he remembered to take a photo for his personal archive. He sat behind the head of the coffin, and as the assistant took the picture, he got so emotional that his eyes filled with tears.

In the church Evgeni spoke with the priest who was to perform the funeral service and learned from him that the church choir was engaged for the ceremony. That set Evgeni's mind at rest.

"Are we expecting a lot of people, Father?" he asked the priest.

"Oh, I doubt it."

"How come?!"

"A few big shots and some celebrities will probably attend, but I don't expect a large crowd. Times have changed."

The priest turned out to be right: a mere seventy people gathered in the church. The Minister of Culture and several celebrities did attend. There were also a few TV crews.

After the funeral, while waiting for the coffin to be loaded into the hearse, Evgeni was surprised by a cable TV journalist, who asked him on camera if it was true that Bulgaria's most famous poet rested in a plywood coffin that cost peanuts. Evgeni denied without going into detail. The journalist said she had it from a reliable source. Evgeni replied there was no more reliable source than himself.

The coffin was carried out of the church and loaded into the hearse, which drove off to the central cemetery. Evgeni headed for his car. At this moment, he was approached by the literary critic who blocked his way asking why he was deceiving the public about the way it was bidding farewell to a great poet.

"Is this about the coffin?" Evgeni asked, smiling amiably.

"About the coffin, yes! And this is not all!"

"The coffin is made of solid wood, sir."

"Here, you're lying again! The coffin is the same as the one shown in your catalog!"

"It's not the same, sir, the coffin is made of solid wood and costs much more than the one in the catalog."

"And who paid for it, if I dare ask? Just don't go telling me the Ministry paid for it!"

"No, sir, the Ministry did not pay for it."

"Who did then?"

"A kind stranger did, sir."

The critic was dumbfounded. He stared at Evgeni's friendly face and didn't know what to say.

"You are laughing!" he said.

"No, sir, I'm just being polite," Evgeni smiled.

"Here you go again..., on a day like this! You are just an insolent bon vivant!" the critic concluded in a spectacular way and walked away with dignity.

Of all the seventy people who attended the service, Evgeni counted fourteen who got to the great poet's grave. Fourteen, no more, no less. They were mostly senior citizens, friends and relatives of the deceased. The critic's eulogy greatly disappointed Evgeni, being dry and uninspired. The critic read it from a crumpled piece of paper in an even, passionless voice. Apparently, when he wrote it, his inspiration had deserted him.

Evgeni stood slightly apart from the group of mourners, thinking with growing sadness that he was witnessing a historic moment that lacked all feeling, let alone solemnity. The handful of people sending off the poetic pride of several generations was no better than if they were burying a hobo. Evgeni gasped for air at this injustice. He waited for the mourners to throw some lumps of earth into the grave and started reciting the poem he had wanted to recite back at the funeral home. His voice was loud and clear, full of inspiration, his head raised to the branches of the trees for the whole world to hear. He couldn't care less about the impression he was making on the mourners. Then, from the corner of his eye, he spotted the critic approaching him. The critic grabbed him by the elbow and hissed:

"Stop it! Stop it this moment! Have you no shame!"

Evgeni was not embarrassed in the least and finished the poem.

In the evening, the family sat in front of the TV to watch the news. All news channels covered the funeral of one of the greatest Bulgarian poets, and some showed video clips of the ceremony.

Suddenly, Evgeni jumped out of his armchair and ran out of the room. His housemates exchanged glances. In a little while, he returned pale as a ghost. In one hand he was holding a book. He sat back in his chair and stared into space. His wife turned the TV off and everyone strained to hear if he was breathing. He was not breathing.

"Breathe, darling, please!" his wife urged him.

Evgeni Sabev had just found out that in the cemetery he had recited not the late poet's verses, but verses written by his recently deceased poetic rival and enemy: another great Bulgarian poet. Evgeni had the two poems mixed up. Instead of reciting the poem of the newly-deceased, he had quoted his rival. It was an insult to the memory of the former, even worse, it was blasphemy. That's why now Evgeni was not breathing and soon the dogs couldn't stand it and started barking.

"Evgeni, darling, breathe please!" his wife urged again and began to lightly slap her husband's plump cheeks.

The following morning Evgeni Sabev didn't get up at five a.m., he didn't wash up, didn't eat, nor sing, and the women slept peacefully until eight. Evgeni had been tossing and turning on the couch all night. At the rare moments he dozed off, the critic would appear in his dream, his words loaded with icy contempt:

"Just an insolent bon vivant!"

In the morning, his wife woke up first and found her husband on the couch. Evgeni Sabev had stopped breathing. This time, for good.

THE YELLOW SUIT

The ethics commission met to discuss the case of Rumyana Hristova, a paramedic at the Emergency Medical Service. The news of the incident she was involved in soon spread across the country: an ambulance transporting a patient with coronary symptoms waited for Rumyana for a good fifteen minutes, while she did some shopping at a nearby store. It was only after her shopping was done that the ambulance with the patient drove off to the hospital.

The ethics commission met urgently because the case had aroused strong public outcry. The commission consisted of five members who had to interrogate Rumyana and come up with a decision. For obvious reasons, the members of the commission were pretty nervous.

At the center of their discussion, as well as at the center of public debate, was the stupefying fact that while the ambulance and the patient were waiting for her, Rumyana Hristova was purchasing clothes. It was also known what exactly she had purchased: a yellow skirt-suit.

After the chairman of the commission opened the meeting, a chubby female doctor spoke up:

"I would understand if, for instance, the paramedic had bought some groceries for home: she didn't have free time and all – been there, done that – but a yellow suit?!"

"Just listen to yourself!" said another member of the commission, an elderly man about to retire. "You're saying that if she had purchased pasta, she would have been innocent!"

"Don't do that, please," the chubby doctor replied peacefully, "don't put words in my mouth."

"It turns out that if you purchase pasta, your guilt is lesser than if you purchase a yellow suit. It remains to be determined what the degree of guilt would be if the suit was not yellow, but, say, blue."

"Or red," added a middle-aged doctor with a wry smile.

"Or red, exactly," the elderly doctor continued, "depending on the color of the ruling party at the time, right?"

"No, no, no, sorry, this is not what I meant. Don't twist my words, please. Fact is, all the media pointedly report that of all things, the paramedic purchased a suit, not something else. Which goes to show... what?"

"What?"

"I don't know! I'm asking you!"

"Why us?!" said a young female doctor with glasses.

"Because you are members of the ethics commission."

"Aren't you?!"

"I am."

"Then you tell us, dear."

"Don't 'dear' me, will you please?"

"I'm just trying to be polite."

"Let's keep it constructive, please," said the chairman of the commission, an elderly man with a big head like a bear. "Where were we?"

"All I wanted to say was," the chubby doctor spoke up timidly, "that Mrs. Hristova bought an item that's not considered a basic necessity."

"Here you go again!" the elderly doctor interrupted. "Let's not focus on a petty detail, please! If you consider pasta a basic…"

"Oh, no, please," protested the chubby doctor again, "I didn't say that!"

"Why are you so obsessed with pasta, anyway?" the doctor with the wry smile said.

"Let's not interrupt each other, please!" the elderly doctor continued. "If for you pasta is a basic necessity, then for our young colleague here maybe a yellow skirt-suit is."

"No, it isn't!" the young doctor snapped.

"Just an example."

"Use other examples, please!" the young doctor said.

"Anyway, let's not focus on petty details!"

"I'm afraid we have no other choice," the doctor with the wry smile intervened. "We are expected to respond to the public attitude. And the public attitude is stirred up by the object of Mrs. Hristova's purchase, which is a yellow skirt-suit. We must, willy-nilly, comply with the public attitude."

"This is no public attitude," said the young doctor, "this is public idiocy, fueled by the media."

"I'll pretend I didn't hear that!" said the chairman of the commission.

"We should be talking about the nature of the violation, not about what Mrs. Hristova purchased."

"In order to talk about the cause of this violation, we must talk about what exactly Mrs. Hristova purchased," said the doctor with the wry smile. "Okay, let me give you another example. How would we have interpreted this case if Mrs. Hristova had walked into a pharmacy to buy Valium?"

"Excuse me?!"

"Valium, yes. Suppose she feared she might have a heart attack coming."

"She's expected to have Valium in her first aid kit, isn't she? Paramedics do."

"Oh, do they? Were you born yesterday, my dear girl? You have no idea how miserable the state of today's ambulances is. Now, imagine Mrs. Hristova senses a heart attack coming and decides she won't be able to take good care of her patient unless she gets Valium, so she goes to the pharmacy across the road to get some. Is this act reprehensible or not?"

The members of the ethics commission did not reply.

"So," the doctor continued, "no matter how we qualify the public attitude, we have to use it as a starting point, meaning Mrs. Hristova's degree of guilt can only be determined after answering the question what exactly she was shopping for while the patient was waiting in the ambulance."

"You can't be serious?!" said the young doctor stupefied.

"I'm always serious."

"In my opinion," the young doctor went on, "it doesn't matter what exactly Mrs. Hristova purchased. The only thing that matters is that she left a coronary patient in the ambulance and went to buy... whatever it was... she took a full fifteen minutes, as a result of which, the next day the patient died in the hospital.

"I totally agree with all you said, except for the line, "as a result of which"," the chairman of the commission interjected. "If the patient had died right away or shortly after he'd been taken to the hospital, then yes. But he died 20 hours after he was hospitalized. Good, we seem to be finally getting somewhere! Now, let's see what Mrs. Hristova has to say."

In a little while, a middle-aged woman entered the room. She was wearing a yellow skirt-suit. She looked pretty scared.

"Are you dressed like that on purpose?" the chairman of the commission asked sternly.

The woman swallowed and said, "No, not on purpose."

"Don't you have anything else to wear?"

"I do, but I wanted to show you what I bought."

"So that we could admire your purchase, is that it?"

"No, not at all!"

"You come here sporting your new outfit, yet you insist you didn't do it on purpose. I don't quite get you?"

"I wanted to show you what I bought as the newspapers wrote it was a suit that cost 300 leva, while, if you take a close look at it you'll see it's an ordinary little suit that costs only 38 leva."

"How do we know that?"

"I've kept the receipt. Here!" The woman opened her purse but the chairman stopped her.

"Mrs. Hristova, I don't care about your receipt. The fact that you've come wearing this particular suit is to your detriment. Furthermore, it's to the detriment of the whole medical profession. You don't seem to be aware of your guilt and your outfit proves it."

"I'm totally aware of my guilt, doctor."

"Were there media people in front of the building?"

"Yes."

"Did they ask you questions?"

"They did."

"What did they ask you about?"

"The suit."

"What about it?"

"The same question you asked: whether I was wearing it on purpose."

"What did you tell them?"

"What I told you: it's not on purpose."

"Why do you insist on everybody knowing how inexpensive this suit is?"

"Because all the papers wrote…"

"Mrs. Hristova, you don't seem to be aware of the gravity of your predicament."

"I am! I promise!" the woman said, bursting into tears.

The room fell silent. The woman fished a tissue out of her purse, dried her eyes and said, "Sorry!"

"Okay," the chairman said, "I'll ask the ladies in our commission to guess the presumptive price of this suit."

The other members of the commission looked at him in astonishment. He winked at them and said:

"Let's lighten up a bit, or Mrs. Hristova won't be able to answer our questions."

The chubby doctor responded to the chairman's invitation and approached the woman, who got up from her chair. The chubby doctor examined the suit closely, felt the material with her hand, and concluded:

"It does look inexpensive, indeed."

"Thank you, doctor!" the chairman said. "Any questions?"

"Mrs. Hristova," the young doctor said, "were you sure the patient had a heart condition, and if you were, in what way exactly did you come to that conclusion?"

"First, I took his blood pressure…"

"Which was…?"

"150 over 100. Ish."

"I beg your pardon?"

"The top number might have been a bit higher, but the bottom did not exceed 100."

"Mrs. Hristova, this reading does not indicate an immediate threat of a heart attack."

"He was not at risk."

"A while ago, you said something else!"

"I didn't. He often calls an ambulance, because he has already survived a heart attack once. I myself was sent to see him three times. He was never in a state of pre-infarction, but as he's afraid of recurrence, he keeps calling us."

"Can anyone confirm your statement that the patient was not in a pre-infarction state, Mrs. Hristova?" the chairman asked.

"His wife can, but she won't: the family is now suing me."

"Well then, why did you decide to take him to the hospital in the first place, when you knew he was not in critical condition?"

"Because if I didn't, he'd start shouting and then he could really bring on a heart attack."

"Did you transport him to the hospital each time?"

"I did."

"Even though he was stable?"

"Yes."

"Mrs. Hristova, you've been working in emergency care for a while and you know there's a shortage of ambulances and teams. Why did you drive a stable patient to the hospital not just once, but a staggering three times?"

"Out of fear, Sir"

"Mrs. Hristova, you are a medic, what do you mean by 'out of fear'?"

"Each time, he'd grab a knife and threaten to kill his wife and me if I didn't take him to the hospital."

"I see! Tell us now, how exactly you purchased this skirt-suit?"

"I saw it in a shop window and since I'd been looking for a suit like that for a long time, I went to buy it as soon as I loaded the patient into the ambulance."

"You took a full fifteen minutes in the store. Did you have to wait in a line?"

"No, but I had to try the suit on, that's what took so long."

"You tried it on?"

"Yes. The small size didn't fit…"

"Mrs. Hristova, do you realize how ridiculous this is?! You have a patient waiting in the ambulance – you claim he is stable, but no one can confirm your statement – and while he is waiting, you are trying on suits in the store? Do you realize that even if the patient was stable indeed, what you did is totally wrong?"

The woman hung her head and said nothing.

"Mrs. Hristova, answer, please! Do you realize that?"

"I do, Sir."

"How would you defend yourself?"

"I can't. Fact is, the man died."

"Can you consider that this might be as a result of your inconsiderate action?"

"It doesn't matter what I say: the man died."

The room fell silent.

"Fine," the chairman went on, "what happened on the way to the hospital? Where were you sitting: next to the driver or in the rear compartment?"

"Next to the driver."

"As you assumed the patient was stable?"

"Yes. But then, suddenly, he began banging on the partition."

"How do you mean?!"

"He was banging with his fists."

"Go on."

"We pulled over, I went to see him and he told me he had left his cigarettes behind so he wanted us to stop somewhere for him to get a pack."

The room went quiet again. The chairman cleared his throat and said, "Go on."

　　　　　　　　　　　　

"We stopped by a tiny corner shop... the basement kind of shops you've got to crouch in front of..."

"And then?"

"Then, he bought some cigarettes. And after that we drove on to the hospital."

"Mrs. Hristova, you allowed your patient to buy cigarettes?!"

"He would have obtained them one way or another," the woman said in a scarcely audible voice.

"Is that so?!"

The woman hung her head and fell silent.

"Go on, please! What happened next?"

"I warned him against smoking inside the ambulance, but he did, just to spite me. When we arrived at the hospital and I opened the ambulance door, it was obvious he'd been smoking and the rear compartment reeked. Then, the hospital staff took over."

It became very quiet in the room. The chairman banged his fist on the table and exclaimed:

"Mrs. Hristova, I am speechless!"

The woman dropped her head guiltily and remained so.

"Did you tell anyone about this cigarette incident?"

"No."

"Why are you telling us?"

The woman looked at the chairman in confusion:

"So that you know."

"Any questions from my colleagues?"

The members of the commission were silent. Everyone stared at the floor.

"Mrs. Hristova, do you indulge everyone that way?" the chairman asked.

The question was lost on the woman.

"Do you spoil everyone in this... absurd way?"

"I spoil my family at home, yes."

"What about your patients?"

"I try my best to make them feel good."

"I don't know what to say to you! I really don't! You are a good woman, but..." the chairman didn't finish off. "Never mind! You may go now. We will summon you again if we find it necessary."

The woman got up from her chair, smoothed down the skirt of her yellow suit and walked out of the room. The fabric her suit was made of wrinkled easily, so her skirt was all creased when she left.

After she was gone, none of the members of the commission said a word.

A CHASE IN THE PARK

In the summer, Mito Mitov's daughter-in-law was hospitalized, and his seven-year-old granddaughter Katerina was left without supervision. Mitov took it upon himself to look after her in the mornings, and her grandma on her mother's side took care of her in the afternoons. Katerina had only one grandmother. Mitov and his ex-wife had split up 22 years earlier.

Recently, the municipality finally renovated the nearby park. They paved the alleys, replaced the benches, put up playground climbers for the kids and started cleaning and sweeping the site regularly. "That's what we've come to," Mitov would comment, "we take sweeping an alley to be like we're building a hospital."

Mitov knew what he was talking about as he used to work for the municipality. He was deputy chief of Civil Defense, but *de facto* he was the boss. The mayor relied on Mitov, not on his boss. Why, you might ask? Because Mitov had brains while his boss had connections, and when asked what seven times eight is, he gave varying answers.

Anyway! Water under the bridge.

Mito's granddaughter Katerina reminded him of his ex-wife. Both had difficult dispositions. At first, Katerina would follow her grandfather's orders, but then she started testing the limits. Mito Mitov did not tolerate insubordination. In his Civil

Defense days he was half-military, at one point he was even issued a hand gun.

Katerina was always playing with dogs, sometimes even
kissing them, rolling around in the dirt and often drinking from
a dubious water fountain that everyone was using, including
said dogs. As a former municipality official, Mitov knew that
the water in Sofia came from many sources, some of which were
straight out hazardous. Katerina had found her grandfather's
weak spot: every once in a while she would run to the fountain
to get a drink; he would chase after her, and soon their walks
turned into constant stalking.

One day, while Mitov was eyeing a young mother, Katerina
drank from the fountain, her grandfather jumped up and slapped
her on the behind, and she fell over as if she'd been beaten to
death. She didn't cry, though. If you hit a person and they don't
cry, it's a sign of insolence. Katerina turned out to be very insolent. Just like her grandmother. When Mitov happened to slap
his wife, she would never cry. Other women would shed a few
tears, just to play the part, but not his wife!

Mitov set out to reeducate his granddaughter. He had
to teach her obedience. For her own good! Or else, she'd get in
trouble. On their way to the park he would try to convince her
of the importance of obedience through illustrative examples.

"Obedience is the most important thing in the world, especially for women. If a man's obedience is as high as Mount Botev,
a woman's obedience must reach that of the highest mountain
peak, Mount Musala."

While delivering this lecture, Mitov was holding Katerina
by the hand, and felt her hand was trying to slip out of his. Mitov tightened his grip to let her know who was stronger. After
seeing who was stronger, Katerina started hopping joyfully with
every step. Mitov put an end to that, too, because, firstly, he was

lecturing her, and secondly, he knew the hopping was a form of protest, and she was doing it to spite him.

Things got even more out of hand in the park. Mitov could not control the happenings there. One day, Katerina hugged a large dog and Mitov started toward her, but she ran away. She was big for her age, even fat, but she ran fast. Mitov hesitated whether he should try to catch her, decided this was a turning point in her reeducation and spiritual development, and darted after her.

He chased her for a while around the park. Mitov ran out of breath and was about to give up, but fortunately Katerina gave up first. He grasped her by the hand and took her back to the bench that served as their base camp.

That's how it got to the point where Mitov slapped her and she dropped to the ground like a sack of potatoes, after which she told her dad that her grandfather was beating her.

"Just let her drink from the fountain, she'll be fine," was his son's verdict.

Mitov's son was a truck driver, who went on long haul drives, was away for weeks and was always starved for sleep. When he was off duty, he slept all day long. The daughter-in-law was sickly, and Katerina was growing up without supervision.

If you're under the impression that chasing and stalking were the only things Mito and his granddaughter did in the park, you're wrong. Every day Mito bought Katerina chips, fruits and something sweet, and lured her to the bench to snack. She was voracious and while she was eating, they talked.

The topics of these conversations varied, but it was during these talks that the real clash between them came to light.

One day, Katerina asked her grandfather what he did for a living. He told her he was retired. She wanted to know what he did before he retired. He said he was a chief. Of what, she asked.

Mito Mitov couldn't think of an answer. How do you explain to a child what Civil Defense is?

After his attempt at explanation, Katerina said:

"I didn't understand a word of it!"

As if she'd heard it from her grandmother.

Whatever Mito would say to his ex-wife, her answer was "I didn't understand a word of it!" Not that she didn't understand. She did, but she wanted to disparage Mito's achievements. "Once a deputy, always a deputy," she used to say. Each time Mito would explain to his wife that the Mayor valued Mito much more than his boss, who was good for nothing and was only the boss *de jure*, while *de facto* Mito was the boss, and his wife would invariably reply, "I didn't understand a word of it!"

Just like her granddaughter now.

Once Katerina asked, "Why are you called Mito?"

"It's the name I was given. Same as you, you're called Katerina, because that's what they named you."

"Katerina is a pretty name, while Mito..." she said and ate a potato chip.

"Mito is a nice Bulgarian name. And you have it as a family name: your full name is Katerina Mitova, don't you like it?"

"I do. What's yours?"

Mito hesitated for a moment, then replied, "My name is Mito Mitov."

She considered that and said, "Well, it's dumb!"

"What's so dumb about it!?"

She did not reply, just ate another chip.

Mito felt the urge to yank the chips out of her hands, but resisted it. His ex-wife, her grandmother, was always on her high horse. On what grounds, nobody knew. When they were married, she refused to take his family name because it was too low-brow, and kept her own – Petrova. Mitova would be low-brow, but Petrova was the highest brow ever! Well, she was on that high horse for a while and in the end eloped with a railroad worker. Anyway!

"A person's name is not important," Mitov said. "What counts is his deeds. You should be proud of your grandfather!"

"Which one?"

"Me!"

"What about the other one?"

"I don't know about him, he's on his own."

"Roumy's grandpa has a Mercedes. Do you have a Mercedes?"

"I have two of them!"

"Liar!"

"Watch it, or you'll get a whooping! Is that any way to talk to your elders?"

Katerina said nothing and ate another chip.

Every conversation they had over snacks would inevitably end in disapproval on Katerina's part.

One day Mitov got fed up and did not buy her a snack, but regretted it as he deprived himself of ammunition, so to speak, lost his means to reeducate. In the following days, he continued to buy her treats which she now had to earn by reciting poems. She knew only one poem, and when Mitov grew tired of it, he made her sing instead. Songs were a different matter: Katerina knew multiple pop folk hits, including the latest ones that Mitov had not heard.

At first, Katerina sang one song per snack, but her grandfather upped the ante to one song per item. You want chips, you sing a song. You want a chocolate wafer bar, you sing another one. Her appetite was so great that she would sing until the bag was empty.

Mitov felt a purely scientific curiosity as to how far her gluttony could go, and one day he filled the bag up to the top.

On that day, Katerina sang a total of seven songs.

"Way to go," Mitov rejoiced, *"that's what I call proper upbringing!"*

The same day an old lady approached them and presented herself, "My name is Elena Lazarova, I used to be a teacher. What you're doing to your granddaughter is disgusting! She's not a dog!"

The teacher walked away with dignity and left Mito Mitov burning with shame.

"What's so disgusting, you bookworm," he told himself later when his shame diminished. *"That I make her sing? She loves to sing, so she sings! Keep your nose out of it, thank you very much! But she's a teacher! Big deal! I am chief of Civil Defense, in charge of the evacuation of the entire population in case of a nuclear war. This is no child's play, it's not enough to know what two times two is and which peak is higher: Botev or Musala."*

The next day, Mitov left Katerina without a snack. She gave him a malicious look and ran to the fountain. After drinking from it, Katerina got completely out of hand: she hugged dogs, kissed their muzzles, ran wild and rolled around in the dirt. Meanwhile, her grandfather sat on the bench in silence. Such was the effect of Lazarova's teaching approach!

At some point, an old man passed by Mito and said, "Why the long face, old timer?"

Mitov did not reply and the man walked away.

Later, Katerina came up to him and said, "I want snacks tomorrow, you hear me?"

At that moment Mitov felt such malice towards his grandchild that it startled him. Fortunately, their walks would soon be over. Katerina's mother was being discharged from the hospital in two days.

Mitov clenched his teeth and brought a snack on the next day, but Katerina refused to sing.

"I'm not going to sing! I'm not a dog!"

"Where have you seen a singing dog?"

"On TV."

"Give us just one song."

"Make me!"

"No snacks then."

"Says you!"

Mito looked around. Their argument had attracted attention.

"Alright," he said and opened the bag.

"Too late! I'm not hungry anymore!" she replied and ran off.

She went to a big shaggy dog and started hugging and kissing it.

Mito got up from the bench, "Katerina!"

She pretended not to hear. He walked toward her, and she started running. The dog ran after her, barking joyfully. Mitov ran after them. He hoped Katerina would give up, but she didn't. He didn't give up either. He was boiling up inside. He'd catch her and give her a good spanking. Enough was enough! A seven-year-old brat was making a fool out of him!

The park had an outdoor café with umbrellas. A young couple with a child was sitting at one of the tables. The woman saw the chase in the park and exclaimed, "Look at that grandpa go, he's so cute! He's chasing his granddaughter!... Oh, the grandpa fell!... Something's wrong!... Rossen, call 911! Jesus! Poor soul! I hope he'll be fine!..."

Mito Mitov had a heart attack and died while running. It all happened so fast that he never felt a thing.

COCKEREL

In his youth, Momchil's father dreamed of working for the armed forces and enrolled at a military academy, but left it prematurely, because he realized the army was not for him. After the academy, he started an aluminum construction materials company, got married and had a son, Momchil. When asked what his father did for a living, young Momchil would proudly answer: he's a hunter!

Hunting ran in the family, and Momchil started joining the hunting party from an early age. At 15 he was already an excellent marksman and shot his first hare. When he turned 18, he got a hunting license and a brand new rifle. The older members of the hunting posse who had known his prematurely departed grandfather, would say Momchil had taken after him.

In the forest, Momchil was in his element. He was a nimble stalker and knew how to build a fire or skin a boar. Even as a young boy, he looked after his father's hunting dogs: they were the most stubborn and courageous in the pack. Momchil had inherited his hunting skills from his grandfather; while from his father – the notion that hunting is not merely chasing and killing wild animals. To kill a wild animal, you have to first grow to love it: that thought might seem outrageous to the uninitiated, but if there is any difference between a hunter and a killer, this is it.

Momchil's father never went straight for the kill during a hunt. It was much more important to him to observe the wild

animals, which he valued more than most humans. Their inno-
cence and predictability, the lack of malice and revengefulness,
the care for their young which in many ways equaled that of
humans, the acts of bravery and self-sacrifice: all of these things
touched and inspired him, and through them he would open his
son's eyes to the richness of nature.

Thanks to his father, Momchil learned to see and hear the
forest, not just to set an ambush. He knew the names of all trees,
the places they liked to grow, the ailments they suffered and the
wood they yielded. At the end of every hunt, when the hunters
sat down to have a drink and exchange tall tales, Momchil would
find an isolated spot and get lost in contemplation.

The silence of the forest was never the same. Sometimes,
when the wind dropped and the birds and insects lay low, Momchil could only hear the light creaking of an old pine tree. During the rare moments of absolute, utter, dead silence, he would
detect – not with his ears, but with some other sense – the breath
of the forest, and become one with it. He'd lie on his stomach and
inhale the aromas. Once, he saw up close a delicate leaf of grass
erupt and scatter its tiny ripe seeds around. The sight was so impressive that Momchil lost his bearings. The eruption produced
by that delicate plant slung him back to the time of the Big Bang.

Momchil's family lived in the suburbs of the capital. To
Momchil, the city was a necessary evil that provided a liveli-
hood for his parents and an education for him. His favorite TV
channel was Animal Planet. He went to school the same way he
went hunting: well prepared. He was disciplined, never late for
appointments. He acted like a man even as a boy: he had a strong
sense of honor and dignity. His role model was his father who
once had admitted that the greatest mistake in his life was the
years spent in the army. The army was not what he had imagined.

Momchil remembered those words and decided to study what he knew and loved. He enrolled at the forestry institute to make sure he was not repeating his father's mistake.

During his freshman year, a new member joined the hunting party: a fatso who turned out to be a former fellow-cadet of his father's from the military academy. Momchil instantly disliked the man – he was loud, insolent and had a habit of patronizing people by slapping their shoulders, or even squeezing their necks. What stunned Momchil the most, however, was the way the newcomer greeted his father, "Oi, Snot, what's up!"

Momchil turned to his father, who looked down and said nothing.

During the entire hunt, Momchil was under the spell of that encounter. He concluded that "snot" was probably a term of endearment in the army. After all, civilians called each other anything ranging from "dickhead" and "bastard" to "bitch" and even "asshole" with friendly smiles on their faces. That hypothesis calmed him, but only somewhat; in his father's place, he would have said something back, otherwise the rest might think it was an insult his father had meekly swallowed.

After the hunt, the newcomer – feeling increasingly popular – informed them that back at the military academy he'd been senior to Momchil's father and would order him around all the time.

"That was the life, eh, Snot? You got teased a little, but hey, that's the army for you."

Once again, his father did not reply but looked away, and Momchil blushed all over. Apparently, "snot" was a name for rookies. Twenty years earlier, life had set these two men on an unequal footing, but now things were different, and Momchil wondered why his father put up with this.

Momchil's favorite novels of chivalry told of olden times when the tiniest speck on a man's honor would lead to physical battle. Momchil believed that his father and he valued honor and dignity more than anything else, and could not understand what made his father keep quiet. He realized that the code of chivalry had its secrets, yet he couldn't ask about them because they were something every man unravels for himself.

During the next hunt, his father was very tense. The hunters gathered near a cornfield, while Momchil's father stood aside, looking like an old lion that has lost the battle and – with it – his place in the pride. Momchil was struck by that comparison.

Meanwhile, the fatso was telling some story to the others. They listened to him as if they had admitted his dominance, which didn't make sense, as the hierarchy in a posse is based on the hunting skills of its members, not on their ability to waste words. The fatso had obviously started hunting out of boredom. He held his new rifle like a stick and had no idea what to do with it. He went hunting for the grub and booze, he would get drunk, blabber nonsense and turn every hunt into a pathetic picnic.

On that day, the hunting party was out for hares. Momchil had never seen his father so intimidated and quiet, and refused to believe that he may be afraid of the fatso.

At the end of that long and painful day, the hunters started laying out the food and drinks, but Momchil and his father headed back to their car, eager to go home. When he saw them, the new ringleader shouted, "Oi, Snot, what's the big hurry!?"

Momchil stopped, turned around and walked toward him.

The weight difference between them was at least 30 kilos. Momchil knew from experience that the outcome of a fight is not determined by the physique or the skill of the participants, not even by their speed, as much as by the ability to go into frenzy and cold-bloodedly focus that energy onto your opponent. Once, he had thrashed a couple of thugs who were harassing a girl on the street. The girl watched in amazement her savior, who looked like a malnourished high-schooler, compared to the two attackers.

Walking toward the brute, Momchil heard his father shout, "Momchil!"

He stopped in front of the fatso and said, "Take that back!"

The man looked at him in surprise, and his face stretched into a smile.

"Look at the little cockerel!"

"Momchil!" his father shouted again, hurrying towards them.

"Take your words back!" Momchil insisted.

"A daredevil!" the brute said to the father. "Your boy has balls, good for him! You sure he's yours?"

If the father had been even a second slower, his son would have charged.

"Stop it!" he commanded, blocking Momchil's way.

By a tremendous effort of will, Momchil withdrew his gaze from the target and returned to the car.

The trip back was painful. The only words that were spoken came from his father, who said, "Never butt in, unless you're asked."

After this incident, the two stopped hunting with the party. Once, they tried to hunt by themselves. The feeling of being outcast was gnawing at them, and they called it a day pretty early.

Momchil wondered what exactly had happened at the military academy over twenty years earlier. His father's silence seeped into their relationship, and whereas before the two could understand each other without words, now the unspoken stood between them. Momchil felt awful for not hunting, mainly because of the dogs. They were in their prime, and it was a pity to watch them waste away at home.

One day, he took advantage of the invitation of a school-mate, and went boar-hunting with him, for the sake of the two dogs.

When they arrived at the rendezvous point, the party had gathered in its entirety. The fatso was standing in the middle, giving a speech, putting on airs. Momchil was looking for an excuse to attack him, but the fatso had realized who he was dealing with, and avoided his gaze, which in the language of animals meant fear.

The dogs were loosed, and so the hunt began.

At first, Momchil and his friend stuck together, but then they lost track of each other. Momchil was listening for the barking of the dogs. At some point, he heard them in the distance and knew they had sniffed out a trail. Soon, they would startle the boars and chase them toward the hunters.

Momchil got into position. While he was waiting, he saw another hunter approaching him. It was the fatso, stumbling around the forest like a tourist.

When he saw Momchil, he froze. The distance between them was too short, but Momchil had no time or intention to leave his spot. The man tried to hide behind a spindly tree, and Momchil smiled. He imagined that the boar, no matter how short-sighted, would inevitably see the fatso behind the tree and find a way around. The barking came in waves: at times it was loud and clear, then it was muffled and distant. Apparently, the boars were trying everything they could to switch direction, but the dogs inevitably herded them back toward the hunters.

Momchil got ready. He knew that sometimes the dogs would stop barking to save their strength. In such cases, the boar could appear within shooting range in almost utter silence, and if you were not ready, you could miss the moment.

The dogs started barking again, and Momchil raised his rifle. Before long the boar rushed out of the distant bushes and headed toward them. A premature shot was heard, followed by a second one. The boar slowed down, while two dogs jumped on its back. It shook them away and darted off with renewed strength. The dogs were tearing at its hind legs, and Momchil dared not shoot, so he let the boar and the dogs run past him.

"Why didn't you shoot, you snot!?" the fatso shouted shrilly, walking toward Momchil.

With a spare move, Momchil aimed his rifle and fired. The buckshot hit the man and he slumped on the ground, then slowly collapsed to one side.

Momchil never took a second look. He knew he had killed him, and went to inform the hunters.

The investigation into the death of the former military man dragged on for two years. The police detective knew everything: that the victim and Momchil's father went to the same academy, that the victim was rude and disrespectful to his former fellow-cadet, and that Momchil once almost started a fight with him. The detective also knew that the victim was terrible at hunting and would often pop up in the wrong place.

Momchil told the investigators that he had fired at the boar but missed, and afterwards it turned out that the victim had come out of his hiding place and stood in the line of fire.

The ballistic analysis, which had to explain how Momchil was aiming at the boar but hit the victim in the head, showed that the victim was standing on much lower ground than the shooter, so Momchil could indeed have shot the man in the head, while aiming at the beast.

The case was brought to court. Momchil was sentenced to two years' probation for manslaughter.

During the investigation, Momchil quit the forestry institute. His father offered him a job at his firm, but Momchil declined and took up a job as an assistant at a friend's car repair shop.

The two hunting dogs were given away to a relative. Momchil and his father never went hunting again. After he started working as a car mechanic, Momchil rented an apartment and moved out.

Those were two difficult years for Momchil's mother. Still, while the investigation was ongoing, she would see him regularly, but after that he stopped visiting his family home. He'd say he was busy. His mother begged him to come see them, on holidays at least, but somehow he always found an excuse.

His mother resigned herself. When she got to missing her son, she would visit him at his place. The two started meeting outside their family home. Outside the home that Momchil had long stopped calling his own.

Fewer and fewer people saw Momchil in public. He'd only leave his apartment for work. He stopped getting together with his friends and acquaintances. He even stopped seeing his high school sweetheart, whom everyone regarded as his future wife. From a thoughtful and serious young man, who could be relied upon for anything, Momchil turned into a textbook recluse. His only company was a lop-eared dog he rescued from the street.

VISITING DAY

Kiro the Boxer's only visitor was his aunt Tsura, who had lost her ID card. Since she couldn't enter the prison building without ID, the visits she paid took place with her out on the street, and Kiro at the tiny window of his cell.

The prison was near the city center. Tsura would stand away from the two-story building, so that she could see her nephew over the high wall. She and Kiro were separated by a street with lots of traffic, and she had to scream at the top of her lungs to be heard over it. The enormous distance and the deafening noise made these visits totally crazy.

Since Kiro's own mother had given up on him, Auntie Tsura was his only visitor, and he was grateful for it. If not for her, he would have lost touch with his folks altogether.

Tsura was so short she looked like a dwarf. Apart from that, she was an ordinary woman with two sons, cousins of Kiro's. During her visits to the prison, she would tell her nephew anything that crossed her mind. The cell faced south and as it got infernally hot in the summer, someone had nailed a sheet of tin across the window to block out the sun. In other words, the cell boasted makeshift blinds, which made it impossible for Tsura to see her nephew. The only thing she could see was Kiro's muscular tattooed arm in the window signaling for "yes" or "no".

Kiro had tried more than once to start a conversation with her. He'd fill his lungs and split the air with his thundering voice.

His cellmates had to plug their ears, but Tsura was either hard of hearing, or she couldn't hear a thing over the noise of the city, and she often answered questions Kiro hadn't asked.

Before he was sent to prison for manslaughter, Kiro had a sweetheart, Zyumbyula. On the very first visit of his auntie, he asked after her.

"How's Zyumbyula doing?"

"Wha?"

"Zyumbyula, Zyumbyula!"

"Can't hear ya, Kiro!"

"Zyum-byul-laaa!"

"Ah, Zyumbyula! I'll say hi for you!"

"Tell her to come!"

"Okay!"

"She have a new lover?"

"I'll tell her you love her, yeah!"

"No! She seeing other men?"

"Can't hear ya! I'll tell her to come, or not?"

"To come!"

Thus the topic of Zyumbyula was exhausted, and Kiro didn't learn a thing.

During the second visit, he broached the subject again, and after they shouted at each other for a while, his auntie said, "Zyumbyula said hi!"

"You told her to come?"

"Yeah, yeah!"

"So?"

"She promised!"

"Why she ain't here!?"

Tsura shrugged.

"She have a new man?"

"Can't hear ya!"

"She getting boned!?"

"Who?"

"Zyumbyula!"

"Ah, yeah, yeah, plenty!"

"Who boned her?"

"Damned if I know!"

"Tell them I'll kill them both!"

"No, it's just the one guy boning her, but I dunno him."

After these attempts, Kiro stopped asking anything. He just listened to his auntie, glad to be in touch with his family.

Kiro the Boxer was strong and savage. His relatives were afraid of him. He'd beat up all of them. The only people he hadn't raised a hand against were his youngest sister Koyna and Tsura. His auntie visited him in prison, but Koyna wouldn't, since Kiro had beaten up her husband a few times. Kiro's relatives celebrated his imprisonment for three full days.

Kiro was lucky to get a cell that was facing the street. Later, he was moved to another cell, and he sank into isolation. Tsura stopped visiting him on account of her missing ID card, and Kiro suddenly knew what it meant to be alone. In utter solitude. Like a dog! He also understood the reason. It was within him.

For the first time in his life Kiro faced his conscience and his conscience passed judgment that he, Kiro the Boxer, was an animal and a murderer. This judgment drove Kiro mad, he thrashed another prisoner and was sent to solitary confinement. Kiro spent a few months in solitary, and since he had no one to beat up there, he grew listless. When it was over, he asked the management to move him back to his former cell, or at least to another one with a view of the street. Otherwise, he explained, no one would come visit him.

The prison management thought long and hard about this, and eventually, on the one hand, punished Kiro by extending his sentence for another year and a half, for recidivism, and on the other hand, rewarded him by moving him back to his former cell. Kiro asked a cellmate to write a letter to Auntie Tsura, informing her that he was back in his former cell.

If someone had told Kiro the Boxer that his life would someday hang on a single visit by Auntie Tsura, he would have died laughing. But there came a day when he really felt like dying. He even started planning to hang himself in the toilets.

On better days, he would see himself as a free citizen working as a garbage man, a porter or a grave-digger. All these dreams ended badly. Kiro knew that sooner or later he would flip out again and go back to jail for beating someone. Why then should he try to become a garbage man, a porter or a grave-digger?

Before he was sent to jail, Kiro did not appreciate the outside world. Now he did, but it was too late. The outside world had conspired to crush him, and crush him it did. And rightfully so. This thought was bugging Kiro the most: the outside world had crushed him for good reason. All of his cellmates blamed the outside world for their fates. Those sentenced for premeditated murder claimed they were victims of court errors. Kiro claimed the same, but since he had no imagination, even he wouldn't buy that. What's worse, he earned himself another year and a half in jail.

Months went by, but Auntie Tsura was not visiting Kiro, and he grew even more listless. He spoke to no one. He didn't feel like eating and started losing weight. His cheeks grew hollow, his eyes were dull and pained. He looked tormented.

One Sunday, when visits were banned for some reason, Kiro happened to look out his window and he saw Auntie Tsura on the street. She was standing there, peering at his window. Kiro froze in surprise.

　　　　　　　　　　　LUDMIL TODOROV

Tsura was waiting to be noticed while her nephew was watching her in a stupor. This could have gone on for a while, but at one point Tsura called Kiro by his name.

Kiro regained his senses and waved to her. She waved back.

"Where ya been, Kiro!? I lost my voice shouting!... I brought boiled chicken and peppermint candy! Left them with the guards!... I got your letter! Radostin read it to me! He said they teach you to write in there! He said you write good!... I went to see your mom and dad! I brought Radostin to read them the letter, but they said no! They send their best, though! Didn't hear the letter, but sent all their best anyway! But hey, that's something, right? They could of sended nothing!... The chicken is from Koyna, the candy is from me!... I saw Zymbyula. She asked about you! Tell him I'll wait for him, she said! Not sure what she mean, 'cause while she is waiting, she's fucking anything that moves, but "tell him I'm waiting for him," she says, and here I am, telling you... Wha? Can't hear ya, Kiro, I'm totally deaf!... But who's to say? She may be waiting and fucking at the same time, it's possible... People don't like you much, Kiro! Only me and Koyna care about you! And Zyumbyula! Maybe. But you must stop beating up people! Little by little, you must learn to not beat people! Take me and Koyna for example: you never beat us. I dunno about Zyumbyula, but if she is waiting, maybe you didn't beat her, too! So turns out, Kiro, you're not that bad! I dunno if you fight each other in there, or maybe they beat you all, I've no idea. But you must think before you hit, Kiro! People are different! Some can take a punch, but that boy you killed, he couldn't, Kiro, and you killed him! You never know if someone can take a punch! Some men are big, but they can't take it! That's why you must think before you hit or better yet: stop hitting at all! You never know who your dealing with!... I didn't mean to tell you, but... Koyna's older boy hit his brother with a slingshot and the little one lost an eye. Your sister cried her heart out, and she beat her older son black and blue, but that won't fix the eye of the little one, right? So, now he's half-blind! I'm off, Kiro. Don't forget about the chicken and the candy!"

Tsura always left abruptly. Kiro had no time to even wave goodbye. He heard almost nothing of what she said. Tsura was a brisk walker, and as soon as she was out of sight, Kiro burst into tears.

His cellmates were dumbfounded.

"Hey, Boxer, what's wrong?!"

Kiro was bellowing like a calf, it was kind of funny. He was hiccoughing and wiping snot away.

"What's wrong?!" his cellmates asked.

Kiro was in no condition to explain. He was hiccoughing and wiping off snot, his cellmates felt sorry for him. They produced a bottle of moonshine and gave it to Kiro. He drank and calmed down.

"Speak now!" they urged him.

"My sister's little one lost an eye."

"How come?"

"Slingshot."

"Who did it?"

"His brother."

His cellmates quieted down while they processed the news.

"The other eye still there?"

"Yeah."

"One eye is better than no eye," the cellmates concluded. "Nobody died."

"Damn right! Nobody died! One eye is better than no eye!"

"Why your crying then?"

"For joy."

"Kiro, no disrespect bro, but you're acting super weird lately! Go beat up someone, you'll feel better!"

HYSTERIA

University Professor Angel Haralanov had a very strange day. When he analyzed it afterwards, he realized that "strange" was a rather mild and belated diagnosis. In other words, this had been his normal kind of day for quite a long time.

The day was bookended by two events. In the morning, the Professor had a scuffle with a driver, and in the evening, he bullied a 7-year-old boy in the entrance to his apartment building. In between, there was a third, smaller misadventure, which did not lead to physical violence, but it could have.

Professor Haralanov was a social psychologist, and had taken a sabbatical to write his scientific work. He would sit down in front of the computer at 6 in the morning, drink his coffee at 10, then go out for a stroll until 11:30, and he would go back home to finish his day's work. He was a distinguished scientist, and several publishing houses were expecting his latest study, to translate it. The book was going well, it was writing itself.

On that autumn day it was drizzling, so Haralanov decided to take his umbrella. Lost in thought, he started crossing a major intersection on a yellow light, which quickly turned red, unleashing a pack of furious cars on him.

Haralanov made a run for it. One of the cars didn't wait and tried to run him over. Haralanov evaded it and even reposted with a light strike to the windshield with the handle of his umbrella. The car stopped. A personable middle-aged man got out of it and attacked Haralanov by grabbing his umbrella and trying to break it.

The umbrella was a British make and remained intact. The two men started shoving each other. Haralanov heard himself utter expletives, the driver responded in kind, the cars around started honking, the drivers rallied around their colleague, and after a brief scuffle everyone moved along.

The incident was so ugly that the Professor grasped at its small mercies. His opponent had been a personable man rather than a garden variety lout. It's one thing to get into a fight with an average lout, but a totally different thing to exchange slaps with a likeable guy. A conflict between nice guys is like a duel, while the physical confrontation between a nice guy and a common lout evokes disgust, and it is to the detriment of the nice guy, because the garden variety lout is disgusting by default.

The second small mercy from the ugly incident was even more important. While he was traversing the local market, making his way between the dog shit and rotten vegetables on the street, the Professor was opening and closing his British umbrella with satisfaction. It had been bent slightly in the skirmish, but even so, when he pressed the button, it smoothly slid open with a pleasant swish.

The drizzle was light, and the Professor folded the umbrella. It seemed unbefitting to use an umbrella when only a few minutes ago he had been cursing like a sailor. Walking towards the nearby park, he analyzed the unpleasant incident.

Clearly, the drivers waiting in the intersection all wanted to run him over. That would be an outlet for the frustration of a population that lived in poverty under the boot of conventional and organized crime, the State and its corrupt institutions. Instead of directing their civil energy toward the criminals, the drivers targeted an insignificant pedestrian. The infantile and cowardly Bulgarian population preferred to punish pedestrians rather than the real culprits for its misfortune.

That brief analysis only confirmed acknowledged truths, and the Professor's train of thought took another direction.

The speed with which he slammed his umbrella on the windshield was impressive. The Professor had not only found time to dodge the car, but also to strike it. Like a fencer, he had stepped back only to pierce his opponent. It was much more important to attack than to defend himself. What is more, at the moment he set foot on the pedestrian crossing and saw the traffic light was yellow, the Professor was already preparing for the attack. He didn't return to the sidewalk, but went forward, knowing all too well that no one was going to wait for him to cross the street. It could even be argued that he was the one, who was looking for trouble and caused the social incident in question.

Lately, the Professor was looking for conflicts everywhere. Once, they used to be conceptual conflicts, big conflicts, significant conflicts related to his work as a scholar and educator, and to his active role in society with opinions that he would voice publicly; while now his conflicts were petty and mundane. The Professor had fits of hysteria. At such moments, his self-preservation instinct stopped functioning. The conflict was more important to him than the question of whether he'd be run over. Only after the conflict could he breathe easily once again.

As if to test him, a large dog approached him in the park. It was a special breed: white, short-haired, with an enormous head. Its owner was roughly the Professor's age, and he was walking the beast unleashed. Once the Professor had witnessed how the white dog jumped on someone's setter and started gnawing at its hind leg. While the setter was squealing in agony, the white dog's owner was lazily telling it to stop, the expression on his face spelling satisfaction. The Professor knew other such owners who used their pet monsters to compensate for their personal and social insignificance. They walked their dogs proudly, flaunting their worthless short-lived superiority over the others.

The big white dog went to the Professor to take a sniff at him. Haralanov shouted to the owner:

"Put your dog on a leash!"

"She's friendly, don't be afraid!"

"Leash your dog right now, I don't want it sniffing at me!"

"Rebecca," the owner called lazily, but the great white beast didn't hear him. Its mind was set on sniffing at the Professor.

Haralanov gripped his British umbrella by the pointy end, swung it around and crashed the handle onto Rebecca's head with all his strength. The dog froze in confusion. Its head was too thick, and it hadn't felt anything apart from the fact, maybe, that it was unwanted company.

"What the hell man!?" the owner shrieked in a surprisingly shrill voice.

The great white beast growled, but wasn't sure what the problem was, or whether there was a problem at all. Haralanov used its confusion to step away. His heart was pounding madly. If the owner uttered a single command, the great white beast would eat the Professor alive in that rainy, desolate park.

Once he was out of harm's way, the Professor opened the umbrella and resumed his walk.

At the age of fifty-five, Professor Angel Haralanov felt an unprecedented surge of intellectual power. He knew he was at the peak of his scientific career. Everything he did yielded fast, high-quality results. He was quick on the uptake in the most complicated of situations and made lightning-fast decisions that would take his fellows months to reach. His intuition enabled him to see the true motivations behind people's actions.

Still, the Professor could not explain what had happened so that his intellectual prowess – capable of overwhelming rectors, ministers and even prime ministers – was now making him wage war with drivers, dog owners and even the dogs themselves. What exactly had happened that he could no longer differentiate between fundamental, significant conflicts and the petty squabbles of senility? What made him invest the same passion in writing an anti-government article and in hitting a dog with an umbrella?

The Professor was an expert in crowd psychology or, in other words, the mob. His cross-disciplinary field of study had made him a polymath in general psychology, psychiatry, sociology, political science, economy, etc. and he was an esteemed analyst, sought after by the politicians and the media alike.

If the general public could see Professor Haralanov in his everyday life, it would be astounded. Once, he raised such hell on the phone with a poor employee of his mobile network operator, that if they released the recording of the conversation, the Professor would be taken into the loony bin.

The park was small, the Professor did laps to prolong his walk. The great white beast and its owner were circling in the opposite direction, and soon the two enemy sides crossed paths again.

The owner had put a leash on the beast. The satisfaction that filled the Professor at the sight of the leash equaled the satisfaction he had felt when his persistent campaign had forced the rector of his university to resign after being exposed as a former snitch for State Security. Those two victories had the same value to the Professor. The rector had ruined the lives of many, the dog was an instrument of human baseness and cruelty, and the Professor did not differentiate between these two.

Passing each other on the broad path, the parties to the conflict exchanged glances. The owner looked offended, and the dog started growling at the Professor. Apparently, it had gotten the message.

Haralanov continued his walk, and suddenly he felt lost in time and space. He lost orientation as to who he was, where he was and what was happening to him. It wasn't the first time he found himself in this strange condition, but as he was overloaded with work, he had always ascribed it to his getting old, and that was that.

It was almost noon, and Haralanov went for lunch to a nearby restaurant that had a delicious menu.

He ordered a potato cream soup, pork with sauerkraut, hot peppers and a pitcher of red wine. With that order, he precluded working for the rest of the day and decided to devote the afternoon entirely to himself.

While he was waiting to be served, he started thinking about senile hysteria. Over time, the human psyche deteriorates and starts overreacting to various stimuli. This was the essence of senile hysteria, in a nutshell.

Now Haralanov reached a different conclusion. His hysteria was the result of knowledge, of experience, of his ability to unravel the true motives of others, to see through the obvious and find a phenomenon, where others would see a mere event. Haralanov had struck the windshield of that car because he had fallen into the trap of a handful of sociopaths who were ready to crush him – both physically and symbolically – as if they were crushing the reason for their miserable lives. He had hit that dog on the head, because by gnawing at the hind leg of the setter, it had brought joy to its owner. Haralanov had raised hell with that poor employee on the phone, because through her the mobile network operator had burst into his home, trying to lure him into another contract. Was it any wonder then that he did not differentiate between a dog and a rector? The rector was an informant, an instrument of State Security, and the dog was a conduit of human cruelty. Which one of the two deserved greater attention?

These conclusions went to show that senile hysteria is a symptom of a rich life experience, of sagacity and even wisdom. Wisdom and hysteria. The mere juxtaposition of these two notions was a scientific scandal in disguise. As a good scientist, Haralanov loved scandals.

His order arrived. The pork shank was excellent. Haralanov wondered where the cook could find sauerkraut this early in autumn, or how he could preserve it since last winter.

The restaurant was warm and very cozy. The Professor ordered another pitcher of wine and some hot peppers. The bread was fresh and tasty. The TV on the wall was muted, while a radio was playing old pop songs.

Haralanov had just reached an important conclusion. Hysteria was the price you pay for your acquired knowledge and wisdom, rather than the inglorious sunset of a meaningless life. When you get to the bottom of things, you don't react like the others. In the sunset of their lives, smart people see the essence. Sometimes the sight is unpleasant and startling.

The Professor left the restaurant in a good mood. He'd lost half a working day, but he'd gained much more. He was armed with a hypothesis that could bring consolation and even hope to the people exhausted and worn out by excessive knowledge.

On his way back home, the Professor was hiccupping from the hot peppers he'd gobbled, and that lifted his spirits even more.

Haralanov entered his apartment building and saw the seven-year-old son of the upstairs neighbors standing by the elevator.

The boy was leaning against the wall and staring at Haralanov without blinking. The elevator was in the upper floors, the button was blinking. Apparently, someone was using it, or the door had jammed again.

"Waiting for the lift?" the Professor asked.

The boy didn't reply. He just stood there, leaning against the wall and staring at Haralanov.

The Professor was pestered by that hyperactive child, who constantly romped about above his head, throwing stuff, stomping and screaming. For hours on end Haralanov would sit in front of his computer, listening to the noises upstairs. He felt as if he lived under a bowling alley. The child's parents, with whom Haralanov had had several talks, promised to take measures, but the child kept on romping.

"Where's your mother?" the Professor asked and hiccupped.

Instead of an answer, the boy uttered a hiccup, too.

"Was that your answer?" the Professor asked and hiccupped again.

The child hiccupped, too.

"Don't do that, it's not polite," Haralanov said, heading for the stairs, but then he hiccupped, and the boy imitated him immediately.

Next, the Professor did something that surprised him as much as the strike on the white dog's head: he reached out, caught the boy by the ear and pulled so hard that the child couldn't even cry out.

"You're a bad-mannered little freak!" he snarled.

The child started wailing, but the Professor pulled at the ear until the boy ran out of breath again.

A moment later, the empty elevator arrived. Stepping inside, Haralanov gave the boy a knuckle on the head, so strong that the boy's knees buckled with pain. Then he entered the elevator, closed the door and pressed the button.

Reaching his home, Haralanov felt the joy that usually filled him after a fit of hysteria. Good thing the elevator came empty. If the boy's mother had been inside, Haralanov could have beaten her, too.

A FIERCE EXPRESSION

Peppi's obsession with not getting screwed over got him into big trouble. Each time he did something good, such as opening the front door for a neighbor loaded with groceries, he got annoyed that instead of thanking him properly, the neighbor just mumbled something, as if it was Peppi's duty to open the door for him. In a fit of rage, Peppi parked his car so that it blocked the neighbor's way out of his garage.

Once, the same neighbor, while getting out of the garage, scratched his car on a tree. Instead of feeling avenged, Peppi got pangs of conscience and offered to paint over the scratch for free. After all, he was a car mechanic. Peppi constantly swayed between the light and the dark sides of his unstable personality. Only on a few occasions did his goodness and his spitefulness balance out, and then he could sleep peacefully.

At the dawn of democracy, Peppi and a friend of his started a car repair shop. The two of them knew about cars as much as their customers did, but the customers at that time had grown up under socialism and dared not complain. Soon, the two friends' business prospered, they hired mechanics, and the money started pouring in. Then, Peppi's partner produced some forged documents and misappropriated his share of the car repair shop. Peppi brought a lawsuit against him, but his former partner bribed the judges and this is where the story ended.

After that, Peppi's life went downhill. His wife left him and he remained alone in the large apartment which was his only acquisition from the golden days of car repair shops in Bulgaria. He equipped his garage with all kinds of tools and spare parts, and began making small repairs replacing batteries and starters, fixing bumpers and brakes: whatever he had learned during his days as an amateur mechanic.

After this downright fraud, Peppi was traumatized and got obsessed with the thought of being cheated. He got so obsessed that he couldn't do anything good for anyone. A while ago, the residents of the building had decided to have a front door with an electronic lock installed. Peppi produced an offer from a friend of his, which made his neighbors suspicious. They found a less expensive offer and accused Peppi of trying to rob them of their money. He accused them of misusing the maintenance funds, and the book-keeper's husband rushed at him to beat him.

Peppi retaliated by damaging the new electronic door. His neighbors called technicians and incurred big extra expenses. Peppi felt avenged, then his conscience reproached him, and one day he said "hi" to his longtime enemy, the book-keeper's husband. The latter replied with contemptuous silence, and Peppi felt cheated and humiliated again.

Now and again, Peppi would bring a woman to his place. He'd play loud music, get drunk and have sex with his visitor. When he got tired, he'd simply kick the woman out. Sometimes, even in the middle of the night.

"I did you a favor," he'd say to the woman in his bed, "I gave you my priceless sperm. What will you give me in return?"

"Don't be mean!"

"Do you deny that I gave you my priceless sperm?"

"I don't."

"How are you going to repay that favor?"

"By never crossing your threshold again!"

"Then beat it!"

"You mean now?!"

"Yeah, what else could I mean?!"

"I'll leave in the morning."

"Better leave now."

"Oh, come on!"

"You may stay longer, but at a certain price."

"Do you want me to pay rent?"

"No, I want you to give me a service."

"What kind of service?"

Peppi would think of some nasty sexual act, and the woman would leave in a jiffy. Before that, she'd ask for cab fare.

"Haha! You'll have to earn it!" Peppi would reply.

One fine day, Peppi became a media star. The municipality increased the garbage tax illegally and Peppi complained on TV. To sound more credible, he lied to the TV people that a protest was being organized in the neighborhood. The TV people asked about the time and the place of the protest and promised to send a crew.

Peppi rounded up his friends in the neighborhood. They promised to take part in the protest, but only three of them showed up at the appointed time. The TV crew was not disheartened at the scarce number of protesters. A female reporter set Peppi up in front of the camera, while the three "protesters" – all of them hung over – blinked stupidly in the background. Peppi spoke for a long time. He was also asked questions from the studio.

Thus, Peppi became a media star. Strangers greeted him on the street. Even his ex-wife called, after years of silence. His neighbors reacted in a funny way: the book-keeper's husband started greeting him, and those with whom he was usually on good terms turned green with envy.

Peppi's friends proclaimed him a hero. The only criticism on their part was that his hair looked disheveled on TV.

"How do you mean, disheveled? I'm almost bald!"

"Exactly!" his critics replied. "Yet, somehow you still looked disheveled!"

"Of course, he would be disheveled!" others defended him, "You can't expect him to apply grease and makeup like those fags in Parliament!"

Peppi did need a haircut, so one day he went to the nearby hair salon.

The woman who usually gave him a haircut had called in sick, so Peppi turned to leave.

"Why are you leaving, Sir?" asked the girl who substituted for the sick hairdresser.

"I am a bit particular, I want Lilli to trim my hair."

"What's particular about you? Apart from being on TV, which I saw and it impressed me to no end!"

"Well, thank you! Thing is, my hair is thinning and I..."

"Come sit down, I'm not afraid of sparse hair."

Peppi sat down.

"What are you afraid of, then?"

"Of daring men."

"Well! Alright then!" Peppi grinned playfully.

One thing led to another, and the girl ended up in his bed.

"Are you a virgin, huh?!" Peppi gaped at her.

She nodded.

"How old are you?"

"Nineteen."

"Boys your age must be blind! Look how pretty you are!"

"Thank you."

"I never thought 19-year-old virgins existed."

"Well, they don't."

"I know, right! So, what were you waiting for?"

"Isn't it clear? For you."

"For me?!" Peppi laughed heartily. "I'm old, my apartment is big, I'll give you that, but my car is a wreck."

"You are not old, and as for the rest, I don't care."

"What do you care about?"

"That you are a real man."

"Well! Who knew! Because of my TV appearance?"

"Yes."

"Nowadays everyone is mouthing off on TV."

"You don't mouth off. I watched you go on camera. They said there was an on-going protest, but there wasn't one. Just three drunkards was all there was to it. It was you alone against everyone else. Those who mouth off, they have mobs behind them to back them up."

Unlike the other viewers of his TV appearance, this girl did not flatter him: she admired him. Her attitude didn't change on their second, nor on their third date.

In bed, she was inexperienced. Peppi soon got fed up with her and made their dates less frequent, but she didn't make scenes like the other women did, just waited patiently to be invited to his home. Everything was different about her, and Peppi began to suspect that her intentions were underhanded. All that nonsense about him being a he-man and what-not, was for chumps. He was neither such a he-man nor anything else to be so proud of. The girl probably had her eye on his apartment.

Peppi decided to break up with her and one night, after sex, he told her to leave.

She wanted to know why.

"Because," Peppi replied.

"Can't I sleep in another room?"

"You can't. This is not a hostel!"

She left without asking for cab fare.

The following day, Peppi got remorseful and went to apologize to her.

She was busy with a client. Peppi had to wait for a while. As he waited, he thought she was deliberately taking a long time, so when she finally approached him, he spoke to her disrespectfully:

"How did you get home last night?"

"By taxi."

"Here, take this money for the cab fare."

"I don't want your money! Listen to me now! If you mess with me again the way you did last night, I will kill you! I will not cry or beg, I will just kill you!" she said, her eyes boring into him.

Peppi lowered his eyes: at that very moment it dawned on him that she loved him. He had never experienced this before. Years earlier, he and his ex-wife got together because the time had come for them to settle down. Their daughter was born, then Peppi lost the car repair shop, and his wife left him. Her decision seemed perfectly rational. Actually, Peppi would've been surprised if she hadn't left.

Things were different now. If the girl had asked for cab fare, Peppi would have easily got rid of her. He kept seeing the fierce expression on her face when she threatened to kill him. No woman had ever threatened to kill him. In cases like this, women usually called him a fag, and that was it.

Peppi knew he was a lowlife, a lout, and a loser. The whole world knew it, except for the girl at the hair salon who was young, inexperienced, and had lost her mind over his TV protest. Young adults are like that: they fly high, then they sober up and the mess begins. Peppi decided to talk to her, but then he got cold feet. He'd never had such conversations. Might as well write her a letter! Sometimes he got mad at this silly girl. Were young men so hard to find and fall in love with?! What she did was sheer extortion! She was trying to screw him over not for material gain, but as emotional blackmail.

Sometimes, he considered sharing his life with her. A stupid idea! Frankly speaking, the girl's admiration flattered him, but if she moved in with him, all his insignificance and pettiness would soon come to light. He was her hero now, but just a few months on, he would turn into an old fart. This prospect seemed to him worse than anything. Now, that would be the worst screw-up ever: to let your hard earned fame slip out like a fart under the bed sheets of family happiness.

For days on end, Peppi was despondent, failing to notice whether someone was screwing him over or not. The little hairdresser had screwed him over so well that everything else, even the lost car repair shop, seemed a mere trifle in comparison. He would recall her expression over and over again, and one day, on his way downtown, he pulled over in front of the hair salon and waited for her to see him.

The girl noticed him and came to the car.

"What are you doing tonight?" he asked.

"I have plans."

"What plans?"

She said nothing, just smiled, and it dawned on Peppi.

"I see!" he uttered shyly. "When should I expect you?"

She thought for a while and said playfully:

"Sometime or other!"

She turned around and walked jauntily back into the salon.

KATYA

Katya had always dreamed of working at the BILLA grocery chain, and more precisely the BILLA supermarket in her neighborhood. She clearly remembered her first visit there as a child, accompanying her father. Katya entered the huge market hall and the sight of it left her speechless. Until then, she had only known the neighborhood grocery and a few childrenswear stores, where her mother would take her. The stories her classmates had told her about BILLA filled her with expectations that turned out to be completely justified and were even surpassed. Her first visit to the supermarket could only be compared to her first trip to the seaside. The innumerable amount of goods in this enormous area, the dignified shoppers pushing carts along the endless aisles, the quiet music, the odd aroma, the coolness of the AC, the bright lighting, and – most of all – the staff in their beautiful uniforms: all of that left its indelible mark on Katya. She wouldn't let go of the cart her father was pushing proudly, as she was afraid she'd get lost. Her eyes wandered and she absorbed everything around her. She still remembered what her father bought on that first day: a loaf of bread, two tins of mackerel, a piece of vacuum-packed cheese, and a large bottle of Coca-Cola.

"You could've bought all that at our grocery store," her mother said when they got home.

"Yeah, right," her father said, "ever seen canned mackerel in our store?"

"Is that why you went to BILLA, to buy canned mackerel?"

"I went to check the prices."

"Well? What are they?"

"Normal."

"Wish you'd done some decent shopping then."

"Shut up! I don't need your advice!"

Katya remembered this conversation, not only because it reminded her of her first visit to BILLA, but also because a few days later her father left her mother for another woman.

In school, Katya didn't do well. She barely finished high school. Overall, she was hard-working, kind, amiable, and the teachers liked her. Her classmates paid little attention to her, though. In the lower grades, Katya felt equal to her peers, she mingled with the other kids, but then something happened and she started losing touch with the community. When puberty hit, the interests of her classmates shifted: the girls began to put on make-up and wear provocative clothes; the boys became louder and more stuck up; everybody smoked all sorts of things and drank heavily, and the teachers could hardly keep them under control in class; disco-clubbing was almost the only topic of conversation, and amidst all this commotion Katya somehow faded out from the picture. No one talked to her, and she didn't talk to anyone, either. She wore whatever, didn't use make-up, didn't smoke, didn't go to discos; she didn't even fit in with the nerds, as she was one of the worst students in the class. You just had nothing to talk about with her.

One might conclude that Katya's dream to work at BILLA sprang up during her first visit there, but this would be wrong: her dream predated the visit. When she saw the supermarket for the first time, it was like she said to herself, *"Aha, so this is what my dream looks like."*

Shortly after she finished high school, a neighbor of hers, who worked as a cashier at BILLA, said the supermarket was hiring assistants to restock the shelves. Several candidates applied and the managers had to choose. It took them two days, and in the meantime Katya didn't lose any sleep, because she knew they would choose her. Which they did.

She set foot in the supermarket with the new, strange feeling that for the first time in her life she was where she belonged. The constant timid smile she wore to appease people was now gone. The well-oiled machine of the large supermarket chain took her into its embrace. She was assigned an instructor. The job was not as easy as it looked. The staff of a supermarket must know the sections inside out, they must replenish stock on the shelves in a certain way, help customers find items they are looking for, be polite to their co-workers, but above all, they must love their job.

Katya's instructor was a short, stocky, middle-aged man. All that was left of his hair was a tiny lock that fluttered on his bald head like a feather. The instructor's face was etched with deep, masculine lines. His fingers were short and stubby. His stocky body was strong enough to easily move anything that got in his way. The moment she saw him, Katya felt butterflies in her stomach.

The instructor let her in on the secrets of the supermarket as if taking her on a journey into a new world with its own laws, order and scent. He spoke little, and Katya absorbed every single word he uttered. Within a few hours he had gained almost full control over her, and had enchanted her so completely, that she began to understand him without a word.

When, for example, he showed her how to arrange the canned beans, she immediately grasped the logic behind his frugal explanations. Packets had to be arranged in a certain way according to size. A pile had to be steady, tidy, customer-firendly and tempting with its proportions.

"There! Beans!" said the instructor and Katya immediately knew what he meant.

The instructor began rearranging a pile of cans knocked down by a clumsy customer, and Katya felt mesmerized, staring at his little stubby fingers without blinking. When he was done with the pile, her face broke into a happy smile.

Katya had never been attracted to men. When she was fifteen an elder boy took her virginity with her consent. Katya allowed him to penetrate her out of curiosity. After this incident, she went on with her life as if nothing had happened.

In the BILLA supermarket, Katya found love, and only then did she realize that love had been dormant in her for as long as she could remember. Her dream of working at BILLA and her dream of loving a man were similar in the fact that only when they came true, did she realize how long she'd been their captive. In both cases, Katya said to herself: *"Aha, so this is what my dream looks like."*

Her first dream was like a palace, and the second one took the shape of a short, bald, middle-aged man who guided her around that palace and revealed its secrets to her.

During the next few days, Katya was overwhelmed by excitement. She was provided with a work uniform, which she took to a seamstress for some alterations. At Katya's insistence, the seamstress raised the hemline to four fingers above the knee: Katya had beautiful legs, and for the first time she decided to show them off. The skirt was too large, so the seamstress made it tighter, so that Katya's bottom stuck out a little, and she was delighted to see she was quite a hottie.

After the first briefing, Katya and the instructor rarely crossed paths. If their eyes accidentally met, Katya's heart would leap up and she'd blush with delight. It was enough for her to see him from afar, transporting goods in a cart, for her heart to start pounding madly. Sometimes she didn't see him for a whole hour. A break that long made her heart tremble with the anticipation of seeing him again.

Katya had always fantasized about the two of them meeting somewhere in the depths of the supermarket, behind closed doors, but as it turned out a rendezvous could take place in public, before everyone's eyes, and still no one was the wiser.

Their rendezvous took place on a twin-step ladder that they were using to replenish the upper shelves of a store section. The instructor called her to give him a hand, and she approached him with no special expectations, as the supermarket was bustling with people.

The instructor climbed up one side of the ladder, and Katya began handing him rolls of toilet paper from the cart on the ground. He was picking the packs up and placing them on the top shelf. As he took each pack from her, Katya felt his hands linger for a moment on hers. It was not until he took the third pack and his hands stayed on hers longer than necessary, that she realized they were having a moment, and her cheeks blushed. A little later, he told her to climb up next to him. She obeyed, and the two of them perched on either side of the ladder.

With an uncharacteristic eloquence, he began to explain something about the upper shelves, where customers could not reach, but could only see what was on display. As he spoke, his hand gripped her around her waist. As a precaution. At one point, he offered her to sit on the top shelf and see things up close.

Katya immediately knew that she would have a problem with her short tight skirt. She looked anxiously down at the customers scurrying between the sections.

"Don't worry, I'll help you," he said, offering his hand.

She climbed up another step, managed to somehow sit on the top shelf, her skirt riding up. He reached out and covered her bare thighs. This gesture was so intimate that Katya froze.

"Don't move," he said, "just watch."

While Katya pretended to be watching, he was doing something else on the shelf below her, and she felt a strong urge to kiss him on the bald head. That's how they spent quite some time: Katya, her legs hanging from the edge of the shelf, and him, a bit below her, busy arranging some items.

Over the next few days, she often smiled at the thought of their rendezvous. Her favorite part was the two of them, perching like birds over the customers' heads: her sitting on the top shelf, and him acting busy underneath, when in fact they were both thinking about each other, enjoying their closeness, and each of them craving to touch the other: she wanted to kiss him on the head, and he – probably to stroke her bare legs.

Katya would often catch herself daydreaming. She imagined him lifting her in his arms and carrying her off someplace. This longing was stronger at night and she began to fear it. Her desire was growing wild, fanning her passions beyond control.

The days went by, and the instructor behaved as if nothing had happened and their rendezvous had never taken place. Katya interrogated her colleague about him, but learned nothing except that he was single. Trying to understand what kind of person he was, Katya began to watch him closely.

It turned out he hardly interacted with his colleagues except for work. He was confident and determined in his work, and mostly silent outside of it. If anyone managed to start a conversation with him, he'd change beyond recognition: he got embarrassed, eyes fixed on the ground, he hummed and hawed and became impossible to talk to. This had Katya totally confused. It took a great deal of wavering before she finally gathered the courage to ask him out for coffee, but he got embarrassed and refused on the pretext that he was busy.

In the morning, he would organize the work of the staff and manage things with such skill and confidence that Katya felt proud of him, but during the breaks he'd become timid and lower his eyes to the ground. The day they both had perched over the customers' heads became far removed in time and almost faded from Katya's memory. She did not for a moment question the romantic character of their rendezvous, but more and more she wondered how it had ever happened in the first place. *"Is this the man who gathered the courage to straighten my skirt,"* she wondered as she secretly watched him sit alone during lunch break. It turned out that the man who had helped with her rebirth was not brave enough to consummate her new self.

Six months passed. Katya gradually got tired of working in the supermarket and decided to quit. Her mother asked her the reason, and when she didn't get a satisfactory answer, she tried to talk her daughter out of quitting. She reminded her that work these days was hard to find. She voiced her disappointment with Katya's lack of perseverence. She reminded Katya that throughout her childhood, her answer to what she wanted to be when she grows up was: a BILLA salesgirl. Her mother also asked if they were happy with her at the supermarket and if any of the managers was harassing her.

When she didn't get a convincing reason, the mother decided Katya was putting on airs. She snapped at her daughter, saying that with her mental abilities Katya could hardly hope for a better job. In the end, she just forbade her to quit.

Had it been a year earlier, Katya would've obeyed her mother, but now she resisted. Her mother realized she had no chance of knocking some sense into her and said:

"Okay, what are you going to do when you quit?"

"Same as you," Katya said. "I want to drive a streetcar."

"You? Drive a streetcar?! Do you have any idea what it takes, missy?!"

Katya's mother was a streetcar driver in the public transport. Quite reluctantly, she signed her daughter up for a streetcar driver training course.

Two instructors were assigned to Katya: one to teach her the road rules, the other – how to drive a streetcar.

During the first lesson, her driving instructor turned the controller of the car with such confidence that Katya felt the butterflies in her stomach once again. The instructor had the same strong hands as the BILLA manager. Yet, unlike him, he was a talkative man, and on the very first day he made a pass at her, touching her backside: not rudely or insultingly, but carefully and with respect. Katya blushed and got so excited she couldn't sleep a wink that night.

Another six months passed. One day, Katya's mother learned that Katya wants to quit her new job.

"No, no way!" said the mother. "Don't let me lose face with my co-workers! What's gotten into you now?! What is it this time? What will you do after that?!"

"I'll take a job as an orderly in a hospital, and then I'll take a course in nursing."

"How did you come up with that?!"

Katya couldn't explain. She couldn't say she was pursuing her dream, because everyone knew her dream was to work at BILLA. In fact, Katya's dream was bigger than BILLA. And even bigger than the streetcar depot she was working at. So, to her mother's question, *How did you come up with that?* she replied:

"Beats me."

"Then, you'd better stay put, girl! You're not going anywhere! Don't you embarrass me in front of my co-workers!"

Katya fell silent. There was no point in arguing.

The same day, she went to the neighboring hospital to enroll as an orderly.

A NEW PERSON

Eva was always late. She was late even for her own wedding. She was late giving birth to her two children, so, both times, the doctors had to induce labor. Eva hated being late. She did her best to be punctual, but she just couldn't be. She was kind of slow to kick off her day: slow to wake up, slow to start work, slow to get angry, and slow to leave or to return. She was like a freight train, both in terms of starting and of stopping: there was no stopping her once she'd been set in motion.

Her colleagues knew this and took advantage of it shamelessly. Eva worked for a large accounting firm. She would take on unlimited amounts of work and would finish it on time. Just like the tortoise in the fable, no hare could outrun her. Eva was often late for work and her boss often threatened to fire her. For a few days following the warning, she would stay punctual, then things would go wrong, and she would start being late again. Her boss, who was an anxious guy, would throw a fit, insult her, but wouldn't fire her as Eva was his best employee.

Eva was a late riser. When they were babies, her children would cry, she'd hear them, but she couldn't muster the energy to get up. Her husband would get annoyed, yelling, *"Some mother you are,"* but with time, he realized Eva was a good mother and got used to her ways. Their children got used to them, too: they would cry till they were blue in the face, then fall asleep exhausted and, eventually, they stopped crying at all.

Eva's movements were slow, fluid, and graceful. She couldn't bring herself to hurry up. No matter how pressed for time she felt from within, from without, she didn't look it. Sometimes, she grew red in the face from hurrying, while at the same time she was finishing her coffee as if in slow motion. Her husband would joke with her:

"Take your time, Eva, no rush."

"I mean... yes... I know..." she'd reply, embarrassed.

"Are the financial reports ready, Eva?" her boss would ask.

"I mean... yes..."

In other words, what she actually meant to say was, *"Last night, I came across some messy miscalculations, I sat up till 2:30 in the morning to put them right, and finally the accounts balanced."*

"Mom, where are my new jeans?"

"Hold on a sec..."

Eva would go to her son's room and find his new jeans, which usually lay on the floor with the rest of his wardrobe. She would rather find the jeans herself instead of saying, *"Look here, all your clothes are on the floor of your room, go find your jeans there."* She found these conversations pointless. They took up her time. When Eva started a conversation, she needed time to finish it.

If the first impression of Eva was that she could not comprehend the simplest things, that wasn't the case. Eva was quick to grasp, but slow to start a conversation. And even slower to start an argument.

"I mean, I don't know... fine, yes... Maybe you're right..."

No matter how confident she was in her own rightness, Eva never expressed a firm opinion. This was due to her inherently delicate nature. *"Maybe you're right"* meant that Eva thought just the opposite. She was too shy to impose her opinion on others, so she would interject words, then sigh, then smile, and eventually blush. Everyone who knew her understood what she was thinking, and those who didn't know her took her for a fool.

Eva's capacity to keep it in was impressive. Still, she had her rare outbursts when something was too much to bear. Her husband had a drinking problem. When he had a few drinks too many, Eva would confront him and say with resentment, "Now, listen to me!"

Then, for a long time, she'd keep silent, her big eyes fixed on him.

The arguments with her son followed a similar pattern. One day, she decided to raise hell with him and led him to his room. When they were alone, Eva said, "Now, listen to me!" And that was it.

Eva knew her son was a slacker, and a conceptual one, at that. For his laziness he'd always provide a bunch of arguments that she couldn't endure to a point where her eyes would fill with tears. On the other hand, his classmates were of the same persuasion, which stopped Eva from judging him too harshly. To top it all, she loved her son to distraction, which was obvious and made it even more difficult for her. Was it any wonder then that all their clashes ended so quickly? The boy knew his mom only too well and being quite devious, he'd give her a kiss at the end of each fight.

Eva's innate sense of justice made her feel unsure. She couldn't readily pass judgment about anything. Her honesty, alongside with her slow reactions, made her easy prey: people would cut in line before her, sellers would shortchange her at the marketplace, her coworkers would manipulate or dupe her, and often even send her on a wild-goose chase. She was fully aware of that, but kept silent, due to some persistent feeling of guilt, kindled by her day-to-day ineptitude. Just like an elephant panicking at the sight of a mouse, she'd fear things that looked trivial at first sight. Once, an incident happened to her on the bus, which threw her off balance for the rest of the day.

Eva knew she was slow, and when using public transport she had to hurry. She tried to be the first one to jump on the bus, so that she would have time to get ready for the ride. She was afraid that if she could not sit down, or at least hold on to something, the sudden departure of the bus would find her unprepared and she'd fall flat on the floor, or even worse, she might push other passengers and knock them down.

On that day, Eva was in luck: the bus opened one of its doors right in front of her and she was the first to get inside, but while she was looking around, all the seats got taken. Eva got herself into a tight spot with a large box containing a toy-truck she had bought for a colleague of hers. The toy-truck was a much sought-after birthday present for her colleague's 5-year-old son.

The bus set off abruptly, Eva lost her balance, bumped her head on the iron railing, and slumped to the floor, still clutching the toy-truck.

She arrived at work an hour late. Her eyes were dull, and when she finally spoke, no one understood her blabbering. At such moments, her voice grew shrill, almost childish.

"They drive as if the buses are loaded with cattle!... It's unspeakable!... Are we cattle?!" she shouted, trembling with anger. Her eyes wandered.

Her colleagues advised her to see a doctor and by noon, the incident was forgotten.

In the early afternoon, the woman for whom the toy-truck was bought, handed her a folder with documents and said she was going home to prepare for her son's birthday party. None of Eva's colleagues in the office thought she could refuse to do a favor for someone. She didn't think it possible, herself, but it was an unusual day, and while her colleague was handing her the folder, Eva said to herself, *"She could at least have asked if I had any spare time."*

At the end of the working day, her boss left two more folders on her desk:

"It's urgent: I need them done by tomorrow!"

At the sight of the three folders, for the first time in her life Eva thought, *"Can I ever get a break?!"*. The only person who would ever feel sorry for her was her seven-year-old daughter Boyana. Eva was about to call her, but gave up. Why bother her? Boyana was old enough and smart enough to sense how her mother was feeling. The two of them were equally slow and over-sensitive, had the same big eyes, and spoke little. They only exchanged glances, full of unceasing love, and smiled at each other silently.

Eva went to the restroom and lit a cigarette, her hands trembling. Her head ached from the bump. She touched the lump on her head and suddenly wished she would die. She wished for a concussion, which would result in a quick death. With one hand she began to splash tap water on her face, with the other, she was still holding the cigarette, and all the while, tears were running out her eyes.

After the working day was over, Eva stayed behind in the office with the three folders. She always tried to put herself in the shoes of the others and help out, but no one would return the favor. She would give, but never get in return. This was so unfair that Eva gasped for air with indignation.

She felt like burning the three folders. She took them to the restroom, held them over the flame of her cigarette lighter, but dared not burn them, so she returned and hurled the folders to the farthest end of the room. She fidgeted about, looking for something to break, something to smash. She grabbed a vase and flung it at the inner glass door. The glass shattered, and Eva sat at her desk, relieved, and took a deep breath.

She left the office at half past one in the morning, without covering up the traces of her outburst. When she returned home, she found her husband sleeping on the couch.

There were dirty plates, glasses and bottles on the small living room table. Eva immediately knew who had paid a visit to her husband: a friend of his who always dropped in uninvited. The two of them would get drunk, and her husband would fall asleep on the couch. He would sleep with his clothes on, covered with a blanket. It was one of the ugliest sights Eva had to put up with.

When she entered the room, her husband opened his eyes, half-sat up, resting on one elbow, and said in an exhausted voice, "Get me some water."

Eva left him thirsty and went to bed.

But she couldn't fall asleep. Her husband had asked for water in a husky, exhausted voice. His hangover condition was obvious, but who could tell whether it was not something more serious.

Eva got up, went to the kitchen, poured some mineral water in a glass and carried it to the living room.

Her husband was asleep. She touched him on the shoulder.

"Here's your water."

"What?"

"You wanted water."

"I drank already. If I had to wait for you..." he muttered and closed his eyes.

"What? What would happen if you had to wait for me?" she asked in an even voice.

"I'd be thirsty all night."

"I see," she said quietly, then her voice suddenly grew shrill. "Get up and drink this water, right now!"

Her husband gave her a startled look.

"You hear what I said?" she went on."Drink this water now!"

"Why?!" he asked sheepishly.

"I'm not answering any questions! I want you to drink up this water right now!"

"Eva, you'll wake the kids..."

"Now! Right this minute!"

"Okay, calm down..."

Her husband took the glass and started drinking from it, his eyes fixed on his wife. When he was half way through, he stopped to rest, but she rushed him again:

"Go ahead! Finish it!"

He forced himself to gulp on.

When he drained the glass dry, Eva grabbed it from his hand and left the living room triumphantly.

Then, she went to bed and promised herself that as of tomorrow she'd be a new person. She'd make people show consideration for her.

The next morning, Eva overslept and was late for work. She hoped her boss would remember having left some extra work for her the night before and wouldn't eat her alive. *"God, I wish he would remember,"* she prayed, *"or I'll have to kill him."* She even knew how exactly she was going to kill him: with that same vase, which was still intact after being hurled the previous night. She would take the vase and give him a crack on the head.

The boss welcomed her with a smile, thanked her for the job well done and handed her another three folders, which were urgent, again. Eva left the folders on her desk, locked herself in the restroom, and spent a long time there, crying. This time she was crying out of gratitude: she thanked God for making people so kind.

LOW F

Klimbo woke up with a muddled head and immediately knew the day was going to be difficult. He looked in the mirror and saw his round, good-natured face and two bloodshot eyes, looking troubled and disoriented. He slowed and deepened his breath, listening to the wheezing in his chest. He opened his mouth to check his tongue, tried in vain to force a cough and left the bathroom. He decided it was too risky to take a shower, as he was going to spend the entire day outside. His schedule was packed: he had meetings, rehearsals and – most importantly – it was his daughter's birthday, and he didn't have a gift yet. He and his wife had agreed on a new cell phone.

His daughter was at school, and his wife was preparing for the party. Klimbo entered the living room and sat down in an armchair, despondent.

"How are you feeling?" his wife called from the kitchen.

"Not good."

"What's wrong?"

"Come check out my eyes."

In a moment, she brought him eye drops.

"My chest is whistling in the key of low F," Klimbo said.

"Come on! I've stuff to do."

"Hear it for yourself."

His wife leaned over half-jokingly, while Klimbo lifted his T-shirt and started breathing in and out.

"You're fine," she said and ruffled his already disheveled hair.

"There!" Klimbo said, "Low F!"

"This is low A," said his wife who was also a musician. "Come grab a bite, I made you breakfast."

Klimbo was a classical bass player, one of the best in the country. He would get invited for all kinds of gigs: jazz, classical music or even pop folk, and he never turned anyone down. How could you refuse in times like these? His wife was a flute player with the orchestra of the national radio. Their daughter was in the heat of puberty: she was easily offended, laughed hysterically, wept for no reason, the works.

"Do we know what model she wants?" his wife asked.

"We do. The most expensive one."

"So...?"

"So, she will have it. Or else, we may find her hanged in the bathroom."

"Stop it!"

Klimbo smiled and started perfunctorily eating his breakfast.

It was going to be a long day with an important rehearsal, followed by a meeting with a foreign impresario, from whom he was expecting a good offer. Meanwhile, he had to buy a phone for his daughter.

On his way to the rehearsal studio, he dropped by the office of two music producers who owed him money. He had yet to receive the humble remainder of a performance fee.

The music company was big, yet it turned out they couldn't come up with Klimbo's 70 leva.

"Are you kidding me?" he grinned.

"Believe it or not!" said the boy in charge of payments.

"Now what?"

"Come back tomorrow."

"That's what you told me last week: to come back tomorrow."

"Well, did you?"

"I am here now."

"Thing is, the cashier only goes to the bank on certain
days. If you come tomorrow, you'll get your money right away."

"Tomorrow doesn't work for me, I need the money today."

"If I had cash on me, I'd pay you out of my pocket and get
it back from the cashier tomorrow, but I don't. Try asking the
producers for it."

"Where are they?"

"Out of the office."

"Okay. I'll go run some errands and be back later."

"Or call me."

"I'm not calling," Klimbo said with a sly smile, "I'm coming back."

From the producers' office, he went to rehearsal. As usual,
he was on time, the rest were late, and the pianist went over the
top. Klimbo got tense, his head was aching and his eyes turned
red. Eventually, he excused himself, saying he had important
business, and left the studio.

He went back to the office where he found one of the
producers. Seeing Klimbo, he said, "Sorry, bro, this is out of my
hands, as you know. You'll have to talk to Rocco."

"Where is he? Call him up."

"It's not a convenient time to call him."

"When will he be here?"

"He's sure to be here, but I don't know when, bro."

"Okay, I'll wait," Klimbo said and sat down.

He called the studio to let them know he'd skip today's rehearsal, took out his phone and surfed the web for a whole hour.

In the end, Rocco did not show up, and Klimbo spoke again with his associate, "I'll run a few errands and I'll be back."

"Better yet, call me."

"I'm not calling, I'm coming back," Klimbo said.

Next, he went to a large electronics store. He knew what phone model he was looking for, but it turned out he was looking for it at a certain price, while the store sold it at quite another.

"Hold on a minute," he said with a smile, "on your website the price is 800 leva, but the price tag here says 850. What gives?"

The shop assistant began explaining, but Klimbo interrupted him, "Don't bother. I know you have the perfect explanation, thank you!"

Outside the store, Klimbo called a friend of his who was familiar with the ploys of the salesmen, and asked him to urgently find the same phone at a more reasonable price. Then he seemed to lose resolve: it crossed his mind that sometimes it's better to simply buy; what's more, he had the money. In the end, he decided to wait for his friend's search results.

There were still two hours left until his appointment with the foreign impresario, so he headed back to the producers' office.

When they saw him coming for the third time, the staff exchanged looks and stifled smiles. Rocco was still out, and Klimbo went to see the associate who was in a meeting.

"I'm back," Klimbo said with a smile, "Where is Rocco?"

"He's out," the associate replied curtly.

"I'll wait for him at the reception."

Klimbo sat down in the waiting room and started browsing the Internet. He expected a quick reply from his friend, and soon he got the call. He gave him an address where the same phone was sold for 650 leva if you got it without the tax.

Klimbo immediately dashed off to the address.

Another surprise awaited him there. Everything his friend had said was true, but due to the high price of the item, they did not keep it in stock, but ordered it on demand and shipment would take 24 hours.

Klimbo knew he had to avoid stress. His stress indicators were the eyes. Before he made up his mind about the phone, he went to the restroom. His eyes were red, but not redder than they had been in the studio this morning. Klimbo did some deep breathing to hear his chest and left the restroom not entirely calm, but at least relieved enough to make this risky yet profitable decision. He put a deposit on the phone and left, trying to put out of his mind what excuse he would give his daughter tonight. She would receive her present with a day's delay, not on her birthday proper.

Klimbo arrived for the meeting with the foreign impresario on time, only to find out from his Bulgarian partners that he had flown off to Frankfurt on urgent business and was sending his apologies. He would make his offer via email. Klimbo was about to say, "Cat got your tongue? Why didn't you call me to cancel the meeting?"

Instead, Klimbo smiled, which was the perfect anti-stress strategy.

Emerging from the meeting place, he saw in a mirror that his eyes were red, but not redder than in the morning. This gave him hope, and he headed for the producers' office.

There, he was told that Rocco had returned, but went out again, and most likely wouldn't be back. Klimbo checked his watch and said he would wait. He sat down in the waiting room and went on the Internet on his phone.

Half an hour passed. At some point, Rocco's associate appeared before him and said, "Step in, bro. I spoke to Rocco, and he brought me up to speed."

They moved to the room next door.

"Rocco said you've received your entire fee… which was considerable, you must agree. We make an exception with your fees, because you are a superb musician. What's with the 70 leva you claim we still owe you?"

"That was the deal," Klimbo said. "You wouldn't transport my bass, so I had to do it myself."

"We don't make such deals. Everyone covers the transport of their own instruments."

"For a trumpet, guitar or saxophone – yes, but an upright bass is different."

"Not really. Same goes for percussions. Miro transported his drums by himself, no extra charge."

"To each his own. Our agreement was for you to pay for the transport."

"Rocco doesn't know about such an agreement."

"Which doesn't mean the agreement wasn't made."

"I'm sorry bro, I just don't get you. You wasted a whole day for 70 leva. I know you are a busy, sought after man. If you ask me, you just lost at least twice as much today."

"Thrice as much, plus a bunch of other things…"

"All right, just don't tell me we must also cover your day's wages!"

"No. I just want my 70 leva."

"Okay, but how did you actually calculate that?"

"That's what my trip cost me."

"A cab fare from your place to the concert hall isn't that much."

"To the hall and back."

"Yes, that's what I meant."

"I didn't transport my bass in a cab. A friend helped me out with his van."

"Why not a cab? The bass fits if you lower the seats."

"Yes, in a hatchback cab."

"Whatever, yes."

"Have you tried to order a cab that is specifically a hatchback?"

"No."

"Try it."

"Okay, but the gas for that van didn't cost 70 leva."

"True. There was rent, too."

"I thought he was your friend?"

"There's no free lunch."

"You're kidding me!"

Klimbo said nothing, just smiled.

"Let's shake on a more reasonable amount – thirty leva."

"Fifty."

"Forty."

"Alright, forty it is," Klimbo said with a wretched look.

The associate produced forty leva and handed the money to Klimbo.

"You are one of a kind, bro! By the way, I've heard you play Beethoven!"

"Brahms."

"Okay, Brahms, what's the difference?"

"A major one."

They laughed and parted as friends.

On his way back home, Klimbo got feverish. He barely got up the stairs and was shivering all over.

The party had started without him. The guests had long arrived: the grandparents of the birthday girl, plus family friends, whose daughter went to the same school as his. Everyone noticed Klimbo's condition and started squawking at him.

"It's nothing, I'm fine," he tried to calm them down.

His wife took him in hand: she led him to another room, brought a thermometer, a blood pressure monitor and a basin of hot water. Klimbo perched miserably on the bed, put the thermometer into his mouth and stepped into the basin to warm his feet.

His daughter came to check on him.

"Sweetheart, you'll get your gift tomorrow, I'm so sorry..." he muttered.

"Don't be ridiculous, Dad, just get better!" she said and gave him a hug and a kiss.

The party went on without Klimbo. He undressed and went to the bathroom to get ready for bed. His chest was whistling either in low F or low A, who knows. His eyes were bloodshot, but at least his tongue was pink as a baby's, the white coating was gone. Factoring in the hard-earned 40 leva, the day hadn't been all bad for Klimbo.

Before he turned in, he opened the wardrobe, took out a shoe box and added the 40 leva to the banknotes inside, which he hadn't counted for a long time and had the urge to do so. But he had to wait until morning, otherwise he risked getting caught counting money on his daughter's birthday. This was mad money, earned in-between things. Not for spending, but for fun. It helped him fight stress.

GIRL TALK

One day, Marietta phoned her friend, Vanya, and invited her over to her place.

Marietta's husband owned two pharmacies and was currently preparing to open a third one, and Vanya, who was a chief architect at one of Sofia's municipalities, wondered what favor would be asked of her. Perhaps some certificate was needed for the new pharmacy, but why the formalities? Vanya and Marietta were close enough to ask each other favors over the phone. If a drug was out of stock, Vanya would call Marietta, whose husband would get the drug for Vanya right away.

Vanya was a super busy woman and hated it when people ate up her time unnecessarily. She could hardly find the time to go to a beauty salon, let alone to have a girl talk. In the hope of saving time, she offered to meet Marietta some place downtown, but Marietta insisted that they get together at her home.

Marietta was notorious for her impressive stubbornness, hidden behind impenetrable looks. When the two of them were at college, Marietta used to take her exams by keeping silent. Somehow, she managed to convince the professors that she did have the knowledge, but was too timid to share it, so they just let her pass. She treated men in a similar way. She wasn't a looker, but she was always surrounded by men. Her coeds wondered how far she was going with these men. Marietta knew how to act mysterious and create an enigmatic aura around herself. Her current invitation was no exception. Vanya couldn't understand why she had to drive all the way to Marietta's place, being overloaded with work as she was.

In the middle of the week, at the end of a long work day, Vanya bought a bunch of flowers and went to visit her friend and former schoolmate.

Marietta had made a cake and the yummy pretzels she was famous for. The two women drank wine and talked about their children. Marietta had a son and Vanya had a daughter. The two friends had given birth to their children in the same year, and now both their children were college freshmen.

Marietta had just started telling something about her son Zhorko, when he came home. After exchanging greetings, Zhorko shut himself in his room. Marietta excused herself and followed him, and Vanya looked around the spacious living room of Marietta's new home.

It was furnished with taste. In one corner there were photos in beautiful wooden frames hung on the wall. Vanya got up to see them and one of them caught her attention.

In the picture, a group of boys and girls posed in the snow in front of a chalet. Next to Vanya was a boy she had a crush on, or maybe even was in love with. The boy liked her too, but things didn't work out between them, because... because the boy hooked up with Marietta instead. It was nobody's fault, it just happened. More than twenty years had passed since then, and Vanya had completely forgotten about it.

Marietta returned from Zhorko's room, poured more wine in the glasses, and said, "Cheers!" The two women clinked their glasses and drank.

"Nice photos," Vanya observed.

"Shall we look at them together?"

"I saw photos from our college years."

"Yes, they are my most precious ones."

Marietta got up from her seat, unhooked the group photo from the wall, and returned to the couch with it.

"Here! See how young we are in this photo."

Vanya took the photo from Marietta and said:

"There were so many of us gathered on that Students Day. There were students from other universities, too. You think we can put names to the faces?"

"The ones from our major, sure."

"I, for one, can't remember this guy."

"Which one?"

"The one standing next to me."

"Well, I don't remember him, either."

"I think he was at our college."

"I wouldn't be surprised."

"Oh, yes, I'm sure we studied together. What was his name?... Let me see. Ah, yes, his name was Boyan, remember him?"

"Vaguely," Marietta replied.

"How come? You guys were dating, weren't you?"

"Me?! Dating him?!... No way!" Marietta burst out laughing.

"Funny. I can even remember seeing you kiss."

"Are you serious?! When?"

"I can't remember."

"Who knew!... You really think so?!"

"I don't know. I might be wrong. If you were kissing you'd remember, wouldn't you?"

"Well, yes, but it's been ages."

"In fact, there were always crowds of men around you, so you might have forgotten it."

"You make me blush."

"Which of the guys in this photo did you date?"

"Oh, my God, are you serious?" Marietta said and grew sullen.

Vanya regretted having started this conversation. The memory of the boy Marietta had stolen from her back then rekindled a long-forgotten suspicion that all of Marietta's acquaintances shared: that Marietta went to bed with every man who happened to cross her path. This suspicion was based on unfounded rumors, but now it flared up anew, and Vanya succumbed to it.

Marietta was sitting up straight on the couch with hands resting on her lap. Expressionless face, dry features, thin lips, boyish physique: a colorless woman if ever there was one. Compared to her, Vanya looked like a Rubenesque beauty. She had a full bosom, juicy lips and smooth curves. The wine had reddened her taut cheeks, and her black eyes glinted provocatively.

The two women sat on the couch in silence. Without realizing it, they got to a point where they didn't know what to say to one another.

Zhorko came to their rescue. He left his room and on his way to the front door, said, "Bye!"

Zhorko found the front door locked. He started fishing for his keys. He did not find them and headed back to his room, but half way there he turned around and stood before his mother:

"Have you seen my keys, Marietta?"

"No."

"You sure?"

"Go study, Zhorko. What part of "go study" do you not understand?"

"The part where you're stealing my keys!" Zhorko retorted.

"You'll get your keys back when you are ready for your exams."

"Is that so?" Zhorko said peevishly, not knowing how to go on. "I can go out without my keys, you know! I can jump from the fourth floor! Do you want me to?!"

"Zhorko, please, auntie Vanya is paying us a visit! We haven't seen each other for ages! Go study!"

Pressed by circumstances, Zhorko headed angrily towards his room. He slammed the door behind him, and his mother smiled apologetically at Vanya:

"I've always wanted a girl. I don't know how to speak to boys."

Vanya felt more and more uneasy in this house. She could share stories of her daughter's disobedience and thus set Marietta's mind at rest, but she didn't feel like broaching that matter right now.

The living room went quiet again.

At one point, Marietta said, "You must be wondering why I wanted you to come see me at home. Well, it's because... I feel lonely and... I am very unhappy."

Marietta broke into tears. Vanya had seen her cry before, but she had forgotten how tiny her tears were.

"My lover ditched me," Marietta said, "and I don't know what to do now."

Vanya stopped breathing.

"He's young, only 32, and I understand. Still... this doesn't make it easier for me."

Vanya was still not breathing.

"He's getting married." Marietta announced and stopped talking.

Vanya took a deep breath and uttered in a scarcely audible voice:

"What about your husband?"

"My husband doesn't know, if that's what you mean."

Vanya needed time to come to her senses.

"Do you get along?" she asked.

Marietta got confused:

"With whom?"

"With Ventzi."

"Oh, yes, I guess." Marietta replied and dried her eyes.

Vanya pressed her hands together tightly to banish the bad feeling that was taking a grip on her. Experience had taught her not to jump to conclusions. Who could tell how things were exactly between Marietta and her husband. Maybe he was cheating on her, maybe they didn't live together.

As if to bring clarity to these thoughts, Marietta said:

"He's very good to me."

Now it was Vanya's turn to get confused:

"Who do you mean?"

"Ventzi."

Vanya thought for a while, then said:

"If I were you, I wouldn't be crying. I'd be happy that I have a good family. Not counting yourself, of course."

That was a joke, but it didn't strike a cord with Marietta, and Vanya felt the old bad feeling overwhelm her again. Throughout her marriage, she had never cheated on her husband, although she had every reason to, as he was constantly cheating on her. And now she was expected to comfort Marietta for splitting up with her young stallion. All this was so unfair that Vanya was on the verge of losing her temper. In an instant, she saw her life in a whole new light. The sight made her dizzy. It turned out she was the most gullible and naive woman in the world, who believed in things that no one else did.

The two women were silent. There was a loud noise of heavy gunfire coming from Zhorko's room. He was venting his anger playing video games.

Vanya stirred and said with effort:

"I've got to go. My folks expect me to make dinner at home."

Marietta took her hand:

"Thank you for coming! I can't tell you how relieved I feel! Thank you so much!"

The two women got up from the couch and walked to the front door.

Shortly before leaving, Vanya suddenly asked:

"Can you really not remember that guy?"

At first, Marietta didn't catch on. Then, she said:

"What guy? The one in the photo? No, I don't remember him, sorry. Should I?"

"No," Vanya said and left.

On the way home, she remembered how much she had liked the guy in the photo and how she had yearned for him. Back then she fervently wanted to get married. It was her time to settle down, as the old say. At first, this memory made her smile, but then she felt such deep sadness that if she hadn't taken a taxi and was sitting next to the driver, she would have burst into tears.

The driver immediately appraised the beauty of the woman sitting next to him and started a chat. Vanya pretended to be listening, while in reality she was thinking hard where to go. She would go anywhere but home, where her husband was.

The taxi drove unimpeded along the deserted streets of the city, and while Vanya was wondering what to do, it pulled over in front of her home. Willy-nilly, she got off, walked into the entrance of the building and realized that she had forgotten to pay the cabby. She rushed back, but the taxi had left. *"Funny,"* she said to herself, feeling relieved. *"How little one needs to come to terms with one's fate,"* she thought. *"An unpaid fare can make things look up. How elementary people are, after all!"*

While Vanya was musing, taking the stairs to put off seeing her husband, the taxi driver thought how ugly it would have been to remind his client to pay her fare. Beautiful women were made to be driven in cars, and all you can do is enjoy their company, not charge them.

INCASTS

The luck of the Kralevs finally turned around. Rado and Venetta Kralev started their own business, and the cash started pouring in. After living day to day for ten strenuous years, they opened a sewing factory, found a market for their production, and their life started humming along.

They bought an apartment in a new building and a new car, they made holiday trips to Greece and started buying icons and other works from the local artists. They had their eye on a country house in a picturesque village some 20 kilometers away from their town.

Over the first few years of their prosperity, the Kralevs were blissful. Then, they were moderately happy. Then, sporadically happy. The family got used to their new status, and life returned to what it used to be before. They didn't worry about heating bills anymore, but money hadn't brought them what they'd expected and hoped for. They didn't know what exactly they were hoping for. They just knew this wasn't it.

Venetta would get annoyed with their best family friends. The man was the manager of the town's postal office, and the woman worked in a bank. The Kralevs' newly-found fortune had not changed the relationship between the two families. Venetta appreciated the Manolovs' lack of envy, but at the same time she was annoyed by it. She found it suspicious that they weren't at least a little bit jealous. It was hypocritical and insincere. Venetta started watching them closely for a word, a glance or a gesture that would betray them.

"They're treating us as if we're still struggling to make ends meet," she complained to her husband. "They pretend they don't see our success. They are trying to disparage our achievements."

Rado was about to object, but then he remembered he had that same problem with his father-in-law.

Before they got rich, Venetta and Rado used to live in a tiny prefab apartment. Their two young sons were entrusted to the care of Venetta's parents. The children lived with their grandparents. Rado and Venetta often visited them, and they always got a hot meal out of it. The Kralevs counted on those meals, as their fridge was always empty.

In the winter, the father-in-law would send Rado to the basement for sauerkraut.

"Go fetch us a head of pickled cabbage, will you?"

Rado would descend to the basement, happy to be useful, he'd grab a head of fermented cabbage from the barrel and bring it upstairs.

So far, so good. But the father-in-law continued sending Rado to the basement even after he'd become one of the most successful businessmen in town.

The first time Rado didn't even pay attention. He only realized what had happened on his way back when a neighbor saw him on the stairs and said:

"Well-well, Mr. Kralev, how's life treating you? Give my regards to your father-in-law!"

That neighbor was a mean gossip. He had always called Rado by his first name, but now he'd addressed him as Mr. Kralev to sting him. There was a rumor going around town that Rado owed his business success to his father-in-law. That was a blatant lie. The father-in-law had in no way contributed to

Rado's financial ascent, apart from helping the young family raise their kids during their times of hardship. But how do you explain that to the town folk? They were just jealous of anyone who was successful in life.

Once, when Venetta's parents were visiting the young family in their new apartment, the father-in-law dispatched Rado to buy him a pack of cigarettes. Now, that was too much! With two grown grandsons at his disposal, the grandpa was sending his wealthy son-in-law for cigarettes.

Rado tried to deflect the order toward his elder son, but the father-in-law said, "Don't send the kid, or tomorrow he'll buy a pack for himself!" So, Rado headed for the store, seething inside.

Venetta was plagued by the hypocrisy of the Manolovs, and Rado – by his father-in-law. That prevented the Kralevs from enjoying their new status. They were one of the wealthiest families in town, yet everyone treated them as before.

Rado and Venetta were always busy. The children had meals at their grandparents' and often spent the night there. The Kralevs owned a large apartment, but the family went on living apart.

"We have no children, you and I," Rado would grumble to Venetta. "How are we different from the people who leave their kids in an orphanage? We aren't! I don't know my own sons, I've no idea who they are, what they like."

"They're fine with Mom. She cooks for them, she watches them, school is close by, they're used to this."

"I'm not talking about your Mom! It's your father who stole our children."

"Don't say that!" protested Venetta, who was too busy to do the housework.

Venetta Kralev made her own patterns for the clothes the factory produced. She had an innate knack for it without having studied fashion design. Once she'd gained some professional confidence, she mustered the courage to take part in a fashion show that was taking place in the capital, at the National Palace of Culture. The show was going to expand her creative and business horizons.

Venetta shared her excitement with the Manolovs. The man muttered a half-hearted "good for you" and the woman told them she once got totally lost in the National Palace of Culture where she went to watch a big pop folk concert in Hall One.

Rado steered the conversation back to the fashion show, asking the dumbest question possible: whether it too was taking place in Hall One. The moron! Whoever makes fashion shows in a hall that seats 4,000 people!? Even in Paris, fashion shows are made for a select few so that the audience can see the new collection up close. Fashion shows are made for connoisseurs, not for the mob!

When they found out the show was not taking place in Hall One, the Manolovs started fretting and consoling Venetta.

"It's alright. Next time you'll make it to Hall One!" the woman said.

Venetta felt the urge to strangle all three of them. She left the living room and kept herself busy in the kitchen for some time until she calmed down.

"They are such hypocrites!" she burst out when their guests were gone. "They are green with envy and they want to belittle our achievements! Oh, she went to a big concert in Hall One, big deal! And you, you're such an ape! Who the hell makes a fashion show for 4,000 people!? How could you ask such a question!?"

"I didn't think it through, I admit, but you should've just told them it was going to be in Hall One. Who cares? They wouldn't know."

"It crossed my mind! I could've rubbed their noses in it, those hypocrites! Oh well, my bad."

Fortunately, the preparation for the fashion show ate up all of Venetta's time, and she forgot about that unpleasant conversation.

The fashion show was a great disappointment. Venetta paid a ton of money in manufacturing costs, participation fee and other expenses, just to see a few models briefly sport her clothes on the catwalk, and that was it. The Kralevs didn't know anyone in these circles, so they couldn't make any useful contacts. After the end of the fashion show, they picked up their stuff and returned ingloriously to their home town.

During their ride back, Rado was reassuring Venetta that it wasn't all that bad and that her participation was an achievement in itself, while she was thinking about the Manolovs. Those ignorant peasants had been right. Now, Nadka would continue to brag about going to a big concert in Hall One, while Venetta would have to keep under wraps an event in which she had invested so much work, money and hopes. Life was so unfair, and for most of their trip back from the capital, she wept.

To cheer her up after the depressing journey, Rado took her to the village where they were planning to buy a country house. It was a winter weekend.

On their way back from the village, Rado entered carelessly into an icy right turn, the car skidded like a sled and rolled over down a slope to the side of the road. The Kralevs were shattered: Venetta broke her right arm and Rado broke his left leg.

They ended up in the local hospital. They paid extra for a private room, made a donation and were given the royal treatment: they ordered off a special menu with a choice of various meals every day.

For the very first time since they had struck gold, the Kralevs felt they were part of the high life. They decided not to worry about a thing. They enjoyed their seclusion, the silence and the special treatment from the staff. They even made love once: Venetta with her plastered arm and Rado with his plastered leg.

Their first visitors were Venetta's parents. When the nurse who had just pocketed a brand new C-note from her patients told them that the parents were there, Rado said:

"We are not available! Tell them we are not available."

"Shall I reschedule the visit?" the nurse asked.

"No. Tell them we'll talk on the phone."

In fact, Rado and Venetta had switched off their cell phones.

The next visit was paid by the Manolovs.

"We're not available!" said Venetta this time around. "Tell them we're not available."

The Kralevs were not available even for their two sons who were sent by their grandmother with a cardboard box of provisions. When the nurse announced their sons wanted to see them, the room grew quiet.

"Those two... deserve a good spanking," Rado said.

"Stop it!"

"They are my biggest failure. I feel queasy just looking at them. We're not available," Rado told the nurse. "Tell them we're not available."

"What about the box?" the nurse asked.

"Tell them to take it back. I wouldn't be surprised if it's full of sauerkraut."

The two boys headed back for their grandparents' loaded with the heavy box.

The Kralevs stayed in the hospital for almost a month, and emerged from it transformed: now they were confident, inaccessible and filled with the dignity that befitted their status. The casts they were put in had straightened Venetta's posture and given Rado a slow, heavy, stately gait.

A RARE BIRD

"I'm a rare bird, although the media seem to have turned their backs on me lately. You have your camera rolling, right?... I'm wearing this tracksuit on purpose. First and foremost, I'm an athlete, and then I'm everything else. My house is messy, you may show it to the viewers, I have nothing to hide from them. On all TV channels, I see identical clean houses – neat and tidy – as if mummies live in them, not people. When you have nothing else to flaunt, you brag about your house. Here, these are all my medals, cups, awards and prizes. Don't set-up the camera in a static position, let me show you around the house, I'm a producer myself, I know a thing or two about filming. You might wonder what I produce? I do ads, video clips, movies, social events, exhibits, concerts, book launches, but my favorite is producing fashion shows. Without being overly modest, mine were the best produced fashion shows in this country, not... you know whose. Come take a look at my wardrobe now... Well? Ha-ha-ha! You're slain, I know! Look at you gape! What did you think when I met you at the front door? You thought I'd ruin your show with my baggy sweats? Don't worry, I won't. There, check this out! How come I have such a posh wardrobe? It's because I am a socialite. For me, these clothes are not a luxury, but a uniform. People don't know that a socialite has many responsibilities. I don't go to receptions and cocktail parties to have fun: I attend them to raise money for charity. I'll tell you where I have a good time.

At home. Are you surprised? Later, I'll show you what I mean. Now, take my professional advice – you can cut it out when you edit the footage – an outfit is a very important thing, but few people know how to use it for a purpose. I put this tracksuit on to fluster you with my wardrobe. If I had dolled up, my wardrobe wouldn't have impressed you. Okay, let's get to the point now... The info about me trading in oil, is true, yes. I started years ago, during the oil embargo on Yugoslavia. Everything was legal, morally reprehensible, but still legal. The embargo was mandatory only for European Union members, while we, the obscure Balkan entities, sold oil to our Serbian brothers. I want to make it perfectly clear that back then, as well as now, no one ever propped me up. I've always been a solo player both on the stadium and in business. I like to be victorious, especially over men. If I told you what kind of men I've crossed swords with, you wouldn't believe it: at some point, half of them just killed each other off. But let's change the subject. These are stories of times gone by. Come see how I enjoy myself. I promised to show you, remember? We'll go downstairs, to the ground floor, it's a little dark there, so you'll need more lighting.

"These here are my rabbits! And these are my pheasants! Take a good look at them because they are rare breeds. I'll feed them on camera. I deliberately left them hungry, so they'd show some activity in the frame. Rabbits eat everything, but they like milk weed the most. In the winter, I buy them vegetables with a heavy heart on account of the vegetables' nitrate content. I try to pick carrots that don't look good, because otherwise they'd be full of nitrates. I feed the pheasants Italian seeds. This is Tobby the rabbit, look how handsome he is! You've never seen a rabbit like that, have you? Truly gorgeous!... Do you appreciate my tracksuit yet? It's a plain old thing, but it has several functions: it says I am an athlete, it serves as a counterpoint to my wardrobe, and it fits in perfectly well with the rabbits and the pheasants. Are we done? All right, go upstairs now, make yourselves some coffee, get some rest, and I'll catch up in a minute. Your idea is to put a day of my life on film, right? Go upstairs, I'll slaughter a rabbit and I'll join you. There's also a surprise for you: I have invited a very famous person to dinner.

"There, we're all set. It took some time, I know! I flayed the rabbit just now, but the pheasant was slaughtered and picked yesterday, because its meat takes time to ripen. I'll start cooking and while I'm at it we can talk. Come again? Really?!... Oh, no! Yes, I see it! What shall I do now? I don't want to change into another outfit, it would be too gaudy. You can remove this bloodstain when you start editing, if you have the right software. You don't? It's a shame! And you call yourselves a big TV network! Well, it can't be helped. I'm going to change. I was planning to change into an evening gown for dinner: that was supposed to make an impact. I'm a perfectionist, you know, sometimes I get obsessed over details, but there is no middle way for me: you either do a job properly, or you half-ass it. I screwed up with Tobby. I held him too close and he spattered me. It's the same Tobby, yes. Anyway. Let's look ahead. I'm going to change. The guest who's coming to dinner is so famous that the viewers will hardly notice my attire. Now, if you'll excuse me. I'll be right back!

"You were asking what I do for fun. Well, I like to invite friends to dinner and cook something nice for them. I rarely invite more than one person at a time, but if it's a couple, I invite both of them. I throw my birthday parties at restaurants. Today, I am preparing two dishes: braised rabbit and stuffed pheasant. You have to know where the meat comes from and what the animals were fed on. What makes my dishes so scrumptious are the sauces and the stuffing. If you want, I can share my recipes with your audience. I never married. I've had a lot of men and zero commitments. As far as I know, I am the only prominent Bulgarian athlete who openly speaks about the way we were interfered with back in the old days. Doping control was very lax and we were being stuffed with all kinds of substances. Anyway, that's history.

"Here I am, in my full splendor! Well? What do you think? Look, baby, if you want your audience to see my stunning garment, you have to use high-key lighting, because the dress is black. Do I have to teach you cinematography? Come here, darling, come feel my thigh! See how firm it is? Solid rock! And my abdomen is even firmer, feel it! These twenty-year-old bimbos have nothing on me! Every day, I spend two hours in the gym downstairs. It's next to the animals' room. Speaking of the animals, I forgot to feed the rabbits! Never mind, I'll feed them with my evening gown on. Rabbits can never have their fill, they are constantly nibbling. By the way, why don't you film me while I feed them in my evening gown? The media have turned their backs on me lately because they consider me an outlier: I don't seem to fit their idea of a lifestyle. Their loss, not mine, I don't need publicity. My dear girl, no matter how persistent you are, I'm not telling you who my guest will be, let's keep his name secret for everyone for the time being. Okay, I'll give you a hint: don't think of a businessman or a politician. Ha-ha-ha, you guessed wrong, but you're close. Ha-ha-ha, no, it's not Stefan Danailov! Keep guessing! In the meantime, I'll feed the rabbits. Come take a shot of me, baby."

PIPSQUEAK

One evening, in one of her idle moments, Patza took the pipsqueak home. He was the brother of one of her friends from the Group, and when he grew up a bit he started coming to their parties, but he didn't drink or snort, and that annoyed the others. Sometimes Patza would doll up and put on her high heels. Once, her heel broke off, and the pipsqueak took her shoe, then briefly disappeared and came back with the shoe mended.

That same evening she took him home to fix her toilet tank. He failed, and Patza said, "You're good for nothing! Let's see how you do in bed!"

When they were done, Patza said, "You're no good in bed, either! What shall I do with you?... Okay, come, I'll give you a lesson."

Patza gave him lessons all night long. She hadn't been with a man for several months. She was thirty-two, and the pipsqueak was twenty.

Patza was a cleaning woman. She lived in the janitor's room of a high rise apartment building in the outskirts of town. Her mother died young, her father drank his way through the family house, and Patza was left homeless. The Group was her second family. Every evening, she would go to the little park by the church, where the members of the Group gossiped, joked and enjoyed each other's company. The love affairs among them were chaotic and short-lived. Sometimes a child was born, and they would bring it up with a joint effort or leave it to the State, as they were drug addicts and their children were sickly.

After he had a taste of Patza's sugar, the pipsqueak started stalking her.

"Go away!" she shouted at him.

"It's about the toilet tank."

"What toilet tank?"

"Yours."

"My tank's just fine, the problem's in your hose!"

Patza's pun was highly appreciated by the Group.

One day, the pipsqueak brought a spare part for the toilet tank. Patza took him home, he replaced the part, and the leakage stopped.

"Good job!" Patza exclaimed. "Let's see what you learned last time!"

When they were done, Patza said, "You didn't learn a thing! You need more lessons."

So he ended up staying overnight once again.

Patza was way too dependent on alcohol and various pills to let herself become dependent on a man. Not that the pipsqueak was a man, but she never allowed even real men into her bed more than three times. If you let someone fuck you more than three times, he starts imagining things, or even beating you. The pipsqueak was not like that, but Patza had rules that she followed to the letter.

The pipsqueak was too easy-going, and the Group didn't like that. Its members often had heated arguments or even fights, and it was never about money, alcohol or pills, but on principle. The members of the Group were free people, full of great personal dignity, unlike the rest of the populace who, in their view, dragged on with their lives like farm animals. The spineless kindness of the pipsqueak annoyed the Group, and Patza was ashamed of him.

Once he came to the park with an old leather satchel. It contained a hammer, a plane, a saw, chunks of wood, nails, wire, dowels.

"I can fix your chairs and the table, they are pretty rickety," he said.

"Go away!" Patza replied and turned her back on him.

That night he waited for her in front of her building, holding the same bag. He was waiting humbly, as if to say, "I'm here, and if you notice me, fine, but if you don't, it's also fine."

Patza had had a few, and she let him into her home for the third time. He got down to fixing the table and the two chairs. She made dinner and produced a bottle of brandy, but he refused to drink yet again.

"Get off your high horse!"

He took a tiny sip from his glass.

"Bottoms up!" Patza ordered, and he obeyed. As a result, he nearly died, and Patza found that so funny that she laughed for a long time, resting her head on the table.

"You can go now," she said after dinner.

He obeyed and started gathering his things. She took pity on him and let him stay over for the third time.

Over the following days, the pipsqueak continued to pester her, so Patza issued a restraining order:

"I forbid you to come closer than 2 meters away from me! If you do, you'll be in trouble! You're no good for me, and I'm no good for you. The fact that I'm friends with your sister doesn't give you any rights."

The pipsqueak obeyed: he'd keep his distance not letting her out of sight.

One day, while she was window shopping at the local mall, Patza saw her suitor following her and started menacingly toward him, meaning to slap him good, but he managed to flee.

In the evening, she complained to his sister, "I can't get rid of him."

"He's dumb, but he's a good kid. Just keep him away, he's very clingy."

Patza's restraining order made things worse. The pipsqueak wouldn't let her out of his sight even for a moment, and one evening she lost patience, jumped off the bench and started pounding his head with her purse.

The Group got agitated. The men stood up and started talking all at once.

"Patza, what's wrong?" one of them asked.

"Nothing," she said, "he's looking at me!"

The man totally flipped out.

"Whatcha looking at, motherfucker!?" he shouted, jumping on the pipsqueak.

The Group chased the pipsqueak away with fists and kicks. The beating they gave him was more unexpected than brutal. The members of the Group were incapable of beating someone brutally: they lacked the strength. During the scuffle, one of them tumbled backward and fell asleep on the pavement.

After this incident, the pipsqueak disappeared from the park.

When he finally returned, the Group greeted him cheerfully. The pipsqueak was wearing new clothes. He sat down next to Patza and said he had gotten a job in construction, making good money, and all that bullshit. Patza was only half-listening to him, but then she realized he was proposing marriage and raised her voice, "I told you to stay away from me, didn't I!?"

　　　　　　　　　　　　　　　　　　　　　

The Group was in a peaceful mood, and a more serious conflict didn't follow. Patza went home angry. She had received several marriage proposals and had even said yes on two occasions, but on the next morning either the suitor didn't remember he'd popped the question, or she didn't remember she'd said yes.

Patza entered her building and saw the pipsqueak waiting for her in the entrance. For the first time, she got scared.

"I'm calling the police!"

"Don't."

"Go away!"

To her relief, he headed out immediately.

"Wait," she called, "come in, we'll talk."

They went inside.

"What do you want from me?"

"I want to marry you."

"I'm old, you're young, forget it."

"You're not old."

"You think so?" Patza said, showing him her mostly missing teeth. "Look!" she said and stripped to the waist.

Her breasts drooped like baby socks. Her skin was bluish, her face was puffy.

"See who you are proposing to!"

Patza opened her toothless mouth again, and the pipsqueak lowered his eyes.

"Go away now," she said.

"When I was a boy, I once saw you at our house. You were so pretty!"

Patza took a deep breath and laughed.

"So, what's your plan? Marry me for the memories?"

"I make good money, I can take care of a family," he went on.

"Yeah, so you said. Go now, don't make me call the police."

He stood silent for a moment, then left.

After that meeting, the pipsqueak stopped going to the park so often.

Once, Patza saw him following her on the street. She stopped walking, and so did he. Patza burst out laughing.

"Won't you stop following me? God, you're so persistent!"

His last attempt to win her over was with a perfume. Patza was in a good mood and accepted the gift. That was the first time she ever saw him smile ear-to-ear. He had good, healthy teeth without a single filling.

"You're just a silly pipsqueak!" she said with affection and ruffled his thick hair.

He was on cloud nine.

After that, the pipsqueak disappeared. His sister got sick and Patza had no one to ask where he was and what had become of him.

Once, she broke her rule to never cry and cried her heart out when she remembered how he'd told her she was so pretty when she was young.

Several months passed, the pipsqueak never came back, and Patza forgot about him.

GENIUS

"If Bulgaria were to produce a genius, it would be a genius of envy," the great Bulgarian writer Yordan Yovkov once predicted.

And it has. I am that genius.

There, I've said it. I must've scored points with the reader. A simple admission is not enough, it must be substantiated. When I was young I wanted to become a writer, and I even won a prize in a short story competition. Then my ideas ran dry, and I was filled with envy toward all my writing brethren. The mere sight of a new book being released immediately filled me with bitterness and disgust. What nerve! To write a book, being as pathetic as you are! So, I was forever filled with hatred for that book, without even having read it.

The envious person is scrawny, skinny. I was like that in my youth: hollow-cheeked and haggard. My envy was bound to turn me into an alcoholic, or a permanently whining loser, until one day I realized it was a gift from above. I was deprived of a writing talent, but I had huge potential for envy, and I had to make the most of it, instead of suffering because of something that was out of my hands.

I am now 45 years old, and I weigh 100 kilos. I'm a professor at a big university. An expert in several fields: literature, printed media, television. I am extremely erudite, I read a lot and I keep track of all new developments. My elevated status allows me the security and confidence to dwell in the dark world of human envy. The difference between the common envier and the genius one is that the former suffers and complains, while the latter finds the inner strength and calm to inhabit these murky landscapes with dignity, and even with delight. Delight is the key word that makes all the difference.

What is the source of that delight? It's the courage to accept the truth about yourself. Happiness can only befall those who stay true to their nature, even if it is disgusting. The adjective *disgusting* is disturbing, isn't it? Well, I have the strength to apply this adjective with no qualms.

But enough insults, let me say something good about myself. Every professor, expert and columnist of my standing can easily fall into the ruts of contented mediocrity. I don't use my high status for easy fame or a high pension, I use it to fulfill my calling in life. I have a rare gift: I can tell if someone has talent by reading just a few lines they've written. I cannot be fooled by their fine style, erudition and significant topics. Nor can I be fooled by the lack thereof. True talent has nothing to do with those. Emily Dickinson described very well how she knew good poetry: it made her whole body go cold. Me, on the contrary, I burn inside as if I've run up ten flights of stairs. My heartbeat quickens. And all of that as a result of reading even a few lines by a talented writer.

The envy that immediately erupts within me makes me literally blind, and I stop reading. I pace across the room, I drink green tea, but never coffee: I've taken my blood pressure at such moments, so I'm careful. When I calm down, I resume reading, and my reactions aren't that acute anymore, unless I come across a rarely brilliant passage.

This begs the question how I can read an entire novel or poetry collection by a talented author without having a heart attack. I must point out that I'm only talking about contemporary

Bulgarian authors, of whom only a handful are truly gifted. Still, how do I finish reading a good book? A defensive mechanism sets off within me. It resembles the thought process of a traffic policeman who has decided to milk you: it doesn't matter that your papers and your car are in order, he will always find reasons to fine you, or even to impound your vehicle.

Thus, after the initial shock of encountering a talented text, I continue reading, bearing in mind that I must find its weakness. After I read through it, I have so many objections that I can say with clear conscience that the text is, okay, not a total failure, but rather insignificant, unimportant. My reading is multifunctional: on the one hand, I think about my health, and on the other, I appreciate the strengths of the text, while hunting for its weaknesses, which I then use to disparage it publicly. Because (here we reach one of the conclusions of my expose) this is my only goal: to devaluate publicly the efforts of talented people. I don't do it out of spite, but rather for humane reasons that I will lay out shortly. First, let's look at the ways I do it.

In this regard, I am a true artist. I always improvise and very rarely repeat myself. I am a sociable person, I know everyone and everyone knows me. I have authority, my opinion matters. Being a saboteur for one season is easy, but it's very difficult to sabotage for years on end without being caught. What do I do when I read a good book? I immediately make an appointment with the author, whom I usually know personally. If he is a debutant, I let him be: it's too dangerous to roast a talented rookie, as you might turn the public against you. I deal with talented rookies at a later stage, when they have grown some muscle and the time is ripe for them to fall victim to the typical Bulgarian backlash toward upstarts.

So, once I've read and liked a new book by a known author, I set up a meeting with him and tell him what exactly I think of his book. Then I tell everyone else the exact opposite: that the book is garbage. When this information reaches the author, he can't and won't believe that people are capable of such duplicity, and often decides that the person who passed on the information is a conniver. In this way I cover up my tracks, and I incite a negative public opinion of a good book. My opinion carries weight, because the arguments I've amassed against the book are thoroughly developed.

On the rare occasions when a truly significant literary work appears on the horizon, I use a different approach: I keep silent about it. If someone asks my opinion, I give a patronizing smile, or even a wink to my interlocutor, who knows that I always have an opinion, and if I cannot be bothered to share it, then something must be wrong with the book. Thus, I devalue the book on the one hand, and on the other, I get credit for being a person who spares authors.

The silent strategy is good, but it's not enough. When a significant book is released, I don't just keep silent about it, I do something more: I write a good review about some hogwash written by an author close to me. The writing crowd can tell that I'm being insincere, but they forgive me, because they know I'm friends with the author. In this way I also score points as a person willing to put his reputation on the line for his friends. However, my ultimate goal is different: to shift the focus of public attention away from the significant book, and direct it toward the bad one, so that my silence about the good book acquires the power to inflict real damage on the gifted author.

Obviously, I rarely write negative reviews. I've done it twice. My goal was to finish off two talented writers at the end of their careers. I wanted to make sure they never recuperated after that. I used the same approach in both cases. I called the two prominent authors up and asked them to give me their books

                    LUDMIL TODOROV

to review them. I could've asked their publishers, which is the common practice, but I asked the authors.

Every good writer knows deep inside how well they've done with their latest book. Both were successful authors past their heyday, and they were pretty nervous. After I asked them for their autographs and said I wanted to review their new books, they were moved by my eagerness and good intentions. I read their books and wrote negative reviews about them. The chilling effect on the two authors was intensified by the fact that I had personally asked them for their books. As if I'd told them, "My dear fellows, I had every intention to write good reviews of your books, but alas, I couldn't find anything good about them." My message was crystal clear: it's high time you stopped writing.

And they did. Neither of them has published anything in years.

Cruel, isn't it? Yes, indeed. But do you want to know what's even more cruel? To be totally deprived of talent. Thus, we come to the true, grand purpose of my activities. I help the ungifted, who suffer all their lives from their mediocrity. I give those people a reason to live. I write good reviews of their bad books, and I wage war against the fortunate, who do not need my support. I harness the energy of my envious soul for a noble cause. I help my untalented brethren any way I can, and that's what distinguishes me from any common envier.

I will conclude with a quote by Goethe, *"I am part of that power which only wills evil and only works good."* It's approximate, but you get the meaning.

Back to writer Yordan Yovkov and his prediction: you tell me if the man was right.

IN MEMORIAM

This week, the host invited only experts to his political show. He was tired of inviting politicians who sounded like parrots repeating the mantras of their party headquarters.

The three guests in the studio were public figures, who appeared on TV quite often, but not often enough to bore the viewers. The first two were political analysts representing opposing political parties, and the third one was a writer. They were going to discuss the civil protests in Bulgaria that drove thousands of people out onto the streets.

After a short intro, the host gave the floor to the first political analyst. He was known for his forthrightness and his ability to analyze the most complicated issues in a way that made them understandable to the general public. Even when he talked over their heads, the audience listened to him and trusted him because he gave them the impression that his ideas were being generated on the spur of the moment. Unlike other analysts, who spoke evenly and dispassionately, this one stammered, acted out, got agitated, waved his arms, and achieved more through his body language than through the power of speech. In the eyes of the audience, he was a man ready to die for his ideas.

The truth is, the first pundit didn't have any ideas to die for. Some time ago, he had traded them for a lot of money and now he belonged to a small circle of people who made up the oligarchic stratum in society.

"What oligarchy?! In Bulgaria?" he would laugh. "An oligarchy exists where there is a functional economy. In this country, even the children know that our economy doesn't work."

When he was asked to come on the show, at first he turned a deaf ear to the invitation, as he didn't give a damn about the on-going civil protests; but when he learned who his opponent would be, he agreed to take part, tempted by the opportunity to frazzle his old enemy in front of thousands of viewers. The two political pundits had been crossing swords on TV, radio and other forums for years and knew each other well.

At the beginning of the show, the first pundit expressed his unreserved support for the protesters on the street and he got so impassioned that he dropped the analysis of the critical situation and went right for the viewers' heartstrings.

"These people don't have money to pay their electricity bills, do you understand what that means?! No, no, you wouldn't understand! That's... monstrous!"

Among experts, this tactic was unacceptable. By ranting about the unenviable position of the people on the street, the first analyst severely limited his opponent's opportunities to get in some rants of his own. When someone rants too long and convincingly enough, their opponent is disarmed.

The second pundit was experienced enough to get out of this situation. He took a gamble by not expressing any sympathy for the protesters, and made a dig at his opponent with a biting remark:

"A thief who cries "Stop thief!". What's more, the thief calls his own theft *monstrous.*"

This, too, was unacceptable among experts, and the first analyst pretended that these words did not refer to him.

The host spoke up:

"Gentlemen, I have invited you as experts, not as politicians. Viewers are tired of listening to politicians, they want to hear analysis, not political attacks."

"No doubt about it!" said the first analyst. "I merely expressed my support for the people on the street, that's all."

"To express support without naming the culprit is demagoguery!" said the second analyst.

"Will anyone name this culprit then?" the host asked.

"Why, of course! The monopolists!" the second analyst replied.

"Now, let's see a short video of the protest rally before we continue from the studio."

As soon as the video started, the second analyst turned to his enemy and said furiously:

"Is this how we're going to play it?"

"Meaning?"

"Dirty!"

"Who started it?"

"You did!"

"Gentlemen, please!" the host interrupted. "I don't understand why you're fighting! Really! Do you understand it?" he asked the writer.

The writer nodded affirmatively, although he did not understand: a writer is expected to understand everything.

When the video ended and the four of them went live again, the first analyst started waving his arms about like a man who would die this minute if he didn't speak out.

"Sorry, I apologize, may I have a word! Just a sentence, a very short one!"

The second analyst tried to stop him, but his opponent began to speak without pausing for a(?) breath and within three minutes he analyzed the current events, proving irrefutably that the country's ruling party was to blame for the crisis.

The second pundit blushed to the roots of his hair. He knew that if he didn't come up with a refutation, his cause would suffer gravely.

Not that he had a cause. He had traded it for European Union democratization grants the moment Bulgaria joined the EU. Now he was dipping into the European funds with both hands, but since his enemy pinned him to the wall with dirty melodramatic tactics, he was forced to roll the dice.

"Everyone knows," he said, "that the oligarchy is the major culprit for our troubles. The oligarchy, which has merged with the government and the mafia structures. Viewers will probably wonder what these structures are. I will now name one of them."

The second analyst named a notorious economic group, widely known as a mafia organization, but he was the first one to gather the courage to publicly discredit it.

This caused a mild shock in the studio. There was radio silence that lasted three full seconds. Then, the host cleared his throat and asked the writer what, in his opinion, the current situation was.

The writer had listened absentmindedly to the two political analysts. While they spoke, he was thinking of his new round-rimmed glasses, which were fashionable among Europe's intellectual elite. He had acquired the unpleasant habit of adjusting them unnecessarily, and now he was careful not to touch them, which led to the host's question finding him unprepared.

In a scattered, postmodernist style, typical of his books, the writer said he understood the people's anger at the high electricity bills, but that this anger lacked the spiritual energy to elevate the protests above the mundane. The spiritual, he said, must take revenge on the political. He continued along this line, using similar binary oppositions such as intimate-public, confessional-performative, and even classical-contemporary. In almost every sentence he'd find a way to drop in the word *meaning*. He did it consciously, because he had read that when you speak in public, it doesn't matter what you say: what matters is how often you repeat a single important key word which the listeners will remember, while everything else will be forgotten within a day.

As he listened to him, the host thought to himself, *"Boy, what a moron."* He hadn't read anything by this author. He trusted his own editors, who claimed that this was Bulgaria's best young writer. *Meaning* this, *meaning* that: his every other word was *meaning*. The host waited in vain for the writer to produce a proper thought. The first analyst couldn't take it and intervened:

"Sorry, I apologize! I've read all your books (this was a lie) and I like them all, but what's the point of talking about meaning, when people can't pay their electricity bills?"

A biting tirade followed, in which the first analyst turned the writer into a laughing stock, but, to everyone's surprise, the victim accepted the attack calmly. He knew that the viewers would remember the compliment of his books and would forget the rest.

The host asked the writer to be more precise:

"Let's try to make it clear to our viewers. Tell us what you see exactly in these protests."

The writer thought for a while, then said:

"I see the people roaming the streets like a lost flock of sheep, and it reminds me of the Treaty of Neuilly, after the signing of which the people were so desperate that they walked the streets aimlessly and with no direction. In the end, they all gathered in front of our immortal author Ivan Vazov's house to seek solace in the great poet.

While he was uttering these words, the writer's eyes filled with tears. The other participants in the show waited for him to draw a conclusion, but he never did.

"What is your example supposed to tell us?" the host asked.

"Let everyone understand it the way they want," was the answer.

"I can explain it," the first analyst intervened again. "The gentleman here illustrated his theories mentioned a while ago: people are lost sheep and only the spiritual leaders of the nation can comfort them. The spirit is stronger than the mundane, and so on. Well, go ahead, comfort them, dear! Maybe you are our present-day Ivan Vazov?"

On hearing these words, the second pundit started laughing out loud.

After publicly exposing the mafia, the second analyst had lost control. *"They could easily beat me to death,"* he thought, *"but I don't think it's in the cards today. Can they really kill me? I don't think so. They are professionals, they know where and how hard to hit so that they don't kill you. Just a beating, big deal, I can take it!"*

The second pundit realized that he had made a good impression on the viewers and had won the dispute with his opponent; despite that, he was tormented by fear. He was in an unstable state of mind: no matter what was going on around him, he was laughing.

"Some show, some experts", the host thought to himself in resentment, counting down the final minutes of runtime.

As the show was drawing to a close, the writer – who was often attacked by detractors for his prose being too sentimental, and even sappy – rested his head on his fist like Rodin's *Thinker* and stayed in that pose till the end of the show. With his glasses of an intellectual and the pose of a thinker, he hoped to correct his image of a sentimental writer.

When the show was over, the first political analyst walked out of the TV building. He had parked his new super expensive SUV in a parking lot a few blocks away, because he didn't want the others to see it. On his way to the parking lot, he analyzed the show. His political enemy had won the match by making an imprudent statement, after which he had literally shit himself out of fear. The fool believed that he was an important actor in the state and feared retribution. No one was going to lay a finger on him, of course. The people he called mafiosos hadn't even heard of him and would let him stew in his own juice and renounce all future public appearances of his own accord.

Meanwhile, the mafia denouncer ordered a taxi on the phone and when the taxi pulled over in front of the entrance, he walked outside cautiously. He examined the dark streets, saw no suspicious people or vehicles, and got into the cab. On the way home, he kept looking around. No one was following him, so he returned home considerably calmed down.

Shortly after parting from his guests, the host suddenly remembered something, which literally made him go numb.

The previous day, protesting in the city of Varna, a young man had set himself on fire. His name still escaped the host's mind. The young man's name was Plamen Goranov, a photographer and an artist, who flared like a torch in front of the municipality building. The host totally forgot about the incident and didn't even ask his guests to comment on this desperate act of self-immolation. The viewers would hardly notice the omission, but the host's enemies certainly would, and they would rub his nose in it, too.

Dammit! He'd expect at least one of his guests to mention Plamen Goranov. Maybe not the political analysts, but certainly the writer! He was supposed to remember, he's a writer, after all!

Thinking about the writer, the host got furious at the self-immolated photographer: instead of devoting his life to a noble cause, he burnt to death. Bulgaria is not Czechia, where self-immolated Jan Palach became an icon for the Czech people. The Bulgarian people are non-believers. Sooner or later, they will disparage Plamen Goranov's self-sacrifice with some excuse of a mental disorder or an incurable disease. Still, his name was worth mentioning. What a shame no one did! Well, too late now.

The host promised himself never to invite the writer to his show again.

The writer, unaware of the host's thoughts and plans, left the building light-headed and in high spirits, and walked along the well-lit night streets of Sofia. His feet, on their own initiative, took him to Ivan Vazov's memorial house. There, he stopped under the great poet's balcony and lost himself in dreaming. *"Maybe you are our present-day Ivan Vazov?"* the political analyst had said in the studio. He said it with irony, but only time will tell who's who.

While he stood under the great poet's balcony, the hope of contemporary Bulgarian literature got so excited that his eyes watered. Before leaving, he bowed to the great poet and returned home with an enlightened soul.

PRINCESS

As a child, Snezhana was often given a good spanking by her mother.

"If I don't slap her, she won't calm down," her mother complained.

Snezhana used to talk back.

"Don't you talk back to me, missy!"

That's how it all usually started, only to end up with a good spanking.

When her mother asked Snezhana to go buy a loaf of bread, saying, "Go buy some bread, sweetie", the child would instantly go fetch the bread. When the request came as an order, Snezhana would start to grumble.

"You are not a princess, you know, and I'm not supposed to beg you for everything, am I?!"

The same thing used to happen at Snezhana's school. If a teacher was strict with her, she would talk back. Her classmates would giggle, and the teacher would ask the disobedient student:

"What was that? Come again?"

"Old fart. Frog. Smurf." She muttered.

Snezhana grew up to be one of the most beautiful girls in town. She had fair skin, blue eyes, a full bosom, and everything else she needed to get hitched. The town boys started making passes at her, but she would only tease them. She got them excited, then held them off, which drove them crazy. In high school, no one managed to steal as much as a kiss from her.

After leaving high school, she put herself on the "pretty girls' market". All day long, she would drink coffee at various joints, in the evening she would go to a disco with the girls, who, one by one, jumped first into the jeeps, then into the lives of the local thugs. Only Snezhana jumped neither into a jeep, nor into anything else.

"Stop hanging out at coffee shops! Settle down!" her mother scolded her. "Or get a job. How much longer are you going to live off me?"

The town they lived in was a big winter resort. Snezhana's mother worked as head housemaid in a hotel and she suggested that her daughter start working with her, but Snezhana refused to work as a maidservant.

"Maidservants no longer exist: now there are chambermaids" explained her mother.

"Same thing," she answered back.

Snezhana's friends got married and she was left by herself. Boredom overtook her, and she considered applying for a job, but there were only service personnel vacancies available in town.

"Well, there are no jobs for princesses in this town," her mother joked.

One joke led to another, and one day she said:

"As of tomorrow, I am stopping your allowance. You won't get pocket money, nor will I buy you clothes any more. You're on your own."

Snezhana had no other alternative but to become a waitress at a hotel restaurant. She didn't care which hotel she would work at, so she chose the one closest to her home.

Her training went smoothly. The hotel manager turned out to be a distant relative of the family. The management treated

Snezhana kindly and she worked as a waitress all through the winter.

She had two kinds of customers: well-mannered and not so well-mannered. The well-mannered ones had to just look her way and Snezhana instantly rushed to their tables, while the others she left hanging: they looked exactly like her mother when she was ordering her to go get bread. They weren't bad people, they just lacked manners. They would often call her at an awkward moment, and if she took too long, they would get irritated, while the well-mannered ones showed consideration and didn't rush her when she was super busy.

Sometimes, the snooty people, as she called them, would drop by the restaurant. Snezhana subjected them to slow torture. For starters, she'd purposely get the drink orders mixed up: she'd serve rakiya to a customer who had ordered vodka, and vodka to the one who had ordered Ouzo. This always guaranteed a most unpleasant start to the evening. Then, she'd take a long time bringing the salads and would finally serve them together with the main course. Thus, the patrons drank their aperitifs without salads, then ordered another round to go with the salad, while in the meantime their food was getting cold. Snezhana would bring them little ice, they'd want more, she'd bring it late and they'd have to drink their cocktails warm.

The snooty people never returned to Snezhana's tables again.

But things didn't always run smoothly. There was this breed of particularly angry, vicious midlife-crisis men who made her life miserable. They came to the restaurant to raise a ruckus. One day, such a man made her reheat his soup, although it was warm enough. Then he made her replace his salad because it didn't look freshly chopped to him. Finally, he blamed her for bringing him orange juice, instead of grapefruit. Snezhana headed for the bar to get another juice and while she was still within hearing distance, she muttered:

"Old fart!"

The man heard her and took her to the Manager.

"Would you repeat what you just called me?"

She didn't, of course.

"Old fart. Your waitress called me an old fart. I insist that you take immediate measures, or else, you can't imagine the hell I'll raise for you."

Customers had complained about her before, and Snezhana barely got away with it this time. She was rescued by her distant relative, the manager of the hotel.

"Did you really call him an old fart, Snezhana?"

"I did," she admitted, "but not to his face."

The manager gave her a tongue-lashing. At the hotel, they taught the staff that the customer is always right, not to mention the fact that the waiters were dependent on the tips they received. Her colleagues would give anything for a small tip, while Snezhana was ready to do anything only if the customers acknowledged her as a human being.

"You're not here to be acknowledged as a human being," her distant relative told her. "It's your duty and responsibility to wait on the customers. And the customers are what? They're always right."

There were customers who'd drop in a good word for her, but on the whole the hotel management saw this as a fluke.

If one could see how Snezhana treated her well-mannered, civilized customers, they would gasp both at the promptness with which she served the tables and at her capacity to remember who ordered what. What's more, she remembered who had eaten what the day before, and if the customer was hesitant about what to order today, she'd discreetly put a word in:

"You had chicken steak yesterday, so wouldn't you like to try our fresh fish today?"

She even went as far as remembering those customers by name. She didn't make a special effort to do so, it just happened. Sometimes, she was heard saying:

"Mrs. Manova, the arugula today looks very good. Would you care for an arugula salad?"

Once, Snezhana heard a customer say about her:

"She knows all our names, can you imagine that?!"

Snezhana's respect for these people was amply repaid. They valued her skills, praised them, and rewarded them appropriately. But such people were very rare.

Snezhana's youth and beauty didn't go unnoticed by the customers, especially by the mature men. They often made passes at her, or even indecent offers, but she kept her cool. If an offer was just delicately hinted at, she even enjoyed it. Snezhana had a mature kind of beauty. She looked like a woman in her thirties. This discouraged her younger admirers. She had a cool kind of beauty and that kept the young hot-blooded guys at bay.

One day, a group of fifteen people came into the restaurant. Among them was the mayor of the town. The men were all wearing suits. It was obvious that they were big fish. The hotel had two stars, but since most of the hotels were closed in the summer, the mayor brought his guests here.

The hotel staff braced themselves to receive the group. In the summer, the restaurant worked with only two waiters: Snezhana and a guy. That day, the man had sprained his ankle and Snezhana was left on her own. This caused panic among the managers.

"Don't worry," Snezhana told them, "I can handle it by myself."

The management hired a trainee waitress to help Snezhana carry the dishes.

Everything went smoothly. Two days later, the head of the hotel called Snezhana to his office to tell her that one of the guests, the manager of the largest and most prestigious five-star hotel in town, was so impressed with her that he wanted to hire her at his restaurant, where the clientele was said to mainly consist of wealthy foreigners and well-to-do Bulgarians.

"I promised him that I'd talk to you, so if you agree, he will take you on first thing tomorrow. You'll make much more money there, so give it a thought."

"But why? What have I done to impress him?" asked Snezhana.

"He liked you, that's all."

"How do you mean he liked me? In what way?"

"See, that's what I thought at first, too, but no, he is a decent man with a family, and he would never put his reputation at risk for an affair with some employee."

"Well, what was it that I did to impress him, then?"

"He said he'd never seen a waitress who could memorize fifteen customers' orders without writing them down, and not make a single mistake throughout the evening. "And mind you," he said, "I have seen many waitresses." He wanted to know how good your English was, but he said it wouldn't be a problem if it wasn't good, he would sign you up for language courses. By the way, how's your English?"

"Good, I guess. I enjoyed studying it."

"Think about it, but fast. I've got to give him an answer tomorrow."

Snezhana took a day to think it over, and then she agreed.

The atmosphere in the new hotel was different, but the work was almost the same. One of the hotel employees checked

Snezhana's knowledge of English, okayed it and Snezhana started working in the restaurant.

Winter came, and the hotel filled up with guests. Snezhana was in her element. The hotel guests were mostly English, German and Scandinavian. Snezhana looked like a Scandinavian girl herself with her fair complexion, blue eyes, round breasts and sturdy calves. The foreigners preferred her to the other waitresses and booked tables served by her. Unlike the Bulgarian customers, they complimented the staff. The restaurant manager regularly praised her on behalf of satisfied customers.

The restaurant was also visited by newly rich Bulgarians, whose demeanor was stiff, they acted self-important and inaccessible. Their voices had a metallic screech to them. Snezhana put up with them not because she was afraid of them, but because she didn't want to disturb the peace of her favorite customers.

A group of Brits once asked her whether her name could be translated into English, and after hearing what it meant, they nicknamed her the "Snow-white Princess", and started calling her "Princess" for short.

"Princess, darling, would you help me choose my dessert, please?"

Back at home, Snezhana, who didn't like bragging even in front of her mother, once said:

"You know what the customers at the hotel call me?... Princess."

THE MALDIVES INCIDENT

At the age of twenty-one, Borko was an inveterate, accomplished liar. Lying is an individual sport like tennis. In lying, as well as in tennis, the earlier you start, the better. Borko started very early, when he was five.

Once, a kid in the neighborhood slapped him, Borko got angry and complained to his cousin, who was his senior, and the cousin beat up the kid. Borko liked the experience of being the center of attention, and before long he lied to his cousin that another kid had hit him. His cousin beat up the other kid, too. Borko was smart enough to change his approach, and whenever he got inspired, he would isolate himself and start shedding tears. His cousin would ask who had insulted him. Borko would keep silent, playing the martyr. Eventually, he'd give out the name of the "culprit" and the cousin would spring into action.

Over the years, Borko developed his gift for lying. He had a rich arsenal of techniques. He acted as if he didn't want to say what he really wanted to say. He told truths arranged in such an order as to produce a big fat lie. He believed his lies and sometimes fell victim to them. Once, he lied to his mother that he had an A in English, and then, for a long time, he was genuinely surprised by his D.

Borko's auntie on his father's side, Bonka, was an old maid. In her early childhood, Bonka suffered from polio and now she limped on her left leg. She loved her nephew to distraction and had devoted her life to him. She worked as chief accountant in a firm. She read a lot, went to concerts, to the theater, and without being intrusive, she mothered Borko. She was a kind, refined woman. Bonka was the only person who would never suspect Borko of lying. She always defended him and supported him in everything. When Borko was still a baby, she started buying him clothes and toys. Then she bought him a computer, then a stereo. She also covered part of the costs of his education in a private high school. And all the while, she was so tactful and resourceful that her brother never felt embarrassed by her help.

From time to time, her brother would reproach her, "You spoil him too much!"

And that was it.

After finishing high school and getting into college, Borko started slacking off. Bonka decided to buy him a car, but her brother objected, and for the first time in her life, she resorted to a lie: she told him that she would give Borko a loan, which he would repay when he started earning a living.

Her brother smiled:

"Do you even believe what you're saying?"

"Nowadays, no young person can do without a car."

"Nowadays, no young person can do without higher education. Do you realize what you are doing? You are going to reward him for dropping out of college." Bonka thought for a moment, then said:

"You might be right! Fine, will you let me make a deal with him: I'll buy him a car in return for his going back to university."

"A deal? With Borko? God, he'll strike a deal with you any time!"

"How do you mean?" his sister got confused.

"He'll make a promise, but he'll never keep it."

"I'm afraid you don't know him."

Borko's father laughed heartily.

"Sweetheart, don't make a deal with Borko! You hear me?! Don't!"

Despite the warning, the deal was made, and Borko bought a new Toyota. Sometimes, he drove his aunt to work, and once he took her to a monastery in the mountains. His aunt was a believer. She went to church every Sunday.

Borko was strictly fulfilling his part of the deal. As soon as he bought himself a car, he started attending college. His aunt was overjoyed.

Several months passed. During one of the Sunday lunches that Bonka invited Borko to, he boasted that he had passed his first exam.

"Studying for studies' sake is stupid" he said. "One must think of one's future. I wouldn't mind starting my own business while I'm studying. I have ideas, but I don't have the money."

"How much is needed?" asked his aunt.

"Ten thousand."

"Euros?"

"Uhh... yeah!"

"What kind of business are you planning to start?"

"Why do you care?" Borko frowned.

His aunt felt uneasy.

"I ask because whatever it is, you may need an accountant. I'm an accountant, after all," she said with a guilty smile.

"Auntie, dear, you're reading my mind! That is the second thing I was going to ask you for: to take on my company's book-keeping... To your other question, the business I want to start has to do with the media."

It was the middle of winter. A month had passed since Bonka had lent the money to her nephew, when one night her brother came over to see her, more dead than alive. He walked into the living room, sat down, and tossed a newspaper on the table.

On one of the pages, there was a photo of Borko and a beautiful girl. The two were kissing against the background of an exotic beach. The newspaper wrote that Borko had stolen some footballer's girlfriend and had taken her to the Maldives. The beauty was said to be a famous model.

"How could you believe a person who is a pathological liar?!" her brother yelled, when he learned who had financed the trip.

That night, Bonka didn't sleep a wink. She had surges of hot flashes. She worried about Borko. Her feeling of guilt was suffocating.

"You gave him twenty thousand leva!" her brother yelled, "To start a business! Are you kidding me!? Bonka, you're totally out of your mind!"

The next day, Bonka went to church and said a fervent prayer. She prayed for Borko, she prayed for him to come out of this episode unhurt, to get himself back on his feet, to continue with his studies, to be well. She prayed for her brother and sister-in-law, too. They, too, were beside themselves.

After skewering her at first, Bonka's brother took pity on her. "Everyone does silly things in their youth," he said, "better to do them in youth than in later life."

Bonka had a wonderful brother and she thanked God for that.

Her brother called every day to see if Borko had dropped in to apologize. Apparently, Borko had promised to visit his aunt, but he didn't keep his promises.

"I'll kill the wretched brat, I'll kill him with my own two hands!" her brother kept raging.

After the Maldives incident, Bonka set out on a process of gaining knowledge of human nature. So far, she had always been well-meaning to people, but now she started looking at them through distrustful eyes. She no longer took things for granted. This weighed on her and she decided to unburden her heart to her best friend, but gave up at the last moment. *I'm a fool to see only the good sides of people, and people are not what they seem; nothing is what it seems. My friend is a gossip and she'll tell everyone about my misfortune.*

"Give an example," another voice whispered within. *"Give at least one example to prove that your friend is a gossip!"*

"Well, for example..."

"Well, for example?"

"Well, for example..."

"You can't, can you? So you have no proof!"

Thus, Bonka lost her bearings and found herself in quick sand. The harder she struggled to get out of it, the deeper she sank. Only in church did she find solace, but even there things went wrong. By questioning nearly everything, she began to question her own faith, and then, things got really frightening.

Her work at the firm was stressful, so Bonka took some days off. She shut herself up at home, started going to church twice a day, and kept crying all the time. At night, she couldn't sleep. She didn't eat and wouldn't let anyone near her. She limped around her apartment like a ghost.

Her whole life, even her faith, was subordinate to her love for Borko. To lose that love meant losing everything. Sometimes Bonka grasped at the failings of others, so that Borko didn't look so bad. This way, things got even more complicated.

With time, she realized that all her life she had been living off her brother. She was a cuckoo in another bird's nest. She had no private life and she had usurped someone else's. She would push and intrude, eager to help and give money.

This thought made Bonka blush. How could she?! How could she ever?!

Her brother called her twice a week. Their conversations were hard to sustain. Her sister-in-law also called, but Bonka didn't find the strength to return any of their calls. Just at the thought of it, she felt shame, which did not diminish with time, but, on the contrary, intensified. How could she?! How could she ever?!

She went to church every Sunday. She had seven more years until retirement.

After the Maldives incident, Borko never went to see his aunt again. She understood. In a way, she was even grateful to him. Erasing her from his life, Borko seemed to be sparing her conscience, while it was screaming and screaming!... How could she, how could she ever?!... Like a lame elephant... stomping around... in people's lives...

HRISTINA

The Berovs were a close-knit family. So close-knit that all of them were crammed into their one-bedroom, while their three-bedroom apartment stayed empty. Hristina and her brother Ivan had always dreamed of moving into the larger apartment and having a normal life, but the years went by, and they never did. Ivan was a detergent supplies wholesaler, and Hristina worked as an office assistant for a foreign company. The two of them shared a room, their parents slept in the living room, and their granny occupied the kitchen.

Their mother often nagged them:

"Why do we have the big apartment, may I ask? Why are we crammed here in this small one? Anyone?"

No one would answer, because it was understood that the big apartment was reserved for the children.

"You'll never get married, the two of you!" she'd scold them. "And it's all my fault! I should just kick you out, instead of putting up with you!"

The mother was a housewife. She and the granny took care of the housework. In the evening the family would gather in the kitchen. It was always fun. Hristina and her father drank together. Ivan, who didn't drink, gained weight. He started going to the gym to keep the extra kilos away.

The family lived on a small street. The apartment was on the second floor, and Hristina kept a close eye on what transpired on the street. She had a playful imagination that enabled her to construct whole pictures from a single detail. Bodies and gestures spoke louder than words. When the Rumyantsevs walked out of the building together and got in their car simultaneously, Hristina knew that all was well between them. If they exited separately, as if the other one didn't exist, this was a sign of tension between them. If the husband gallantly opened the door for his wife, they had recently made love, but if she was walking in front of him shaking her booty, they hadn't had sex for a while and she was prepping him for tonight.

Sometimes Hristina would strike gold. Once, she saw the car of another neighbor pass by its usual parking spot and turn around the street corner. Soon, the neighbor returned on foot, which meant he had parked somewhere else. That piqued Hristina's curiosity, and she decided to watch what would follow. The neighbor entered the building.

Dusk was falling. People were passing by on the street, but Hristina's attention was fixed on the corner. Before long, a young woman appeared there, and Hristina focused on her. The young woman reached the entrance to the building and quickly stepped inside. She was a stranger.

Hristina remembered she hadn't seen the neighbor's wife for a while, and she asked her mother where she was.

"She's on a business trip to the UK," her mother said, and everything fell into place.

The neighbor was cheating on his wife, and that was a real find, because they were regarded as one of the model families in the building. If someone had asked Hristina why she was sure the young woman was visiting that very neighbor and not someone else, she'd have replied, "Because she entered the building quickly, with her head down, like someone who knew the way but didn't want to be seen."

In front of Hristina's window there was a tall tree that blocked her view, so every spring she asked her father to trim it. He always cut the branches right down to the trunk, to the outrage of the neighbors who couldn't understand why he was trimming the tree instead of enjoying its shade.

Ivan and Hristina kept their love lives secret. When someone asked them a question about intimate partners, they'd always dodge it with a joke. Every now and then Hristina went to the large apartment to check on her brother's love life. It was a known fact that he brought his dates there. Hristina's inspections were like police investigations. She walked around the apartment with her hands clasped behind her back.

Ivan was aware that his sister was spying on him and always covered his tracks. Hristina always knew when he'd brought a woman to the apartment, but she couldn't always prove it. Once, she peeked inside the trash bin in the bathroom and saw a ball of hair, left after the combing ritual of a long-haired woman. That find made Hristina laugh out loud. Her brother was supposed to be a master cover up artist, but he hadn't checked the most obvious place!

As to Hristina's own love life, she definitely had one. She had occasional one-night stands. Once, even a three-night stand. She had a pretty face, but her build was heavy, and she felt clumsy in bed. What's even worse, she always ended up with scrawny men: lean, skinny and elegant. She wished she could find someone in her own weight class! Hristina knew that weight was not everything in an affair, but the other elements were missing, too. She didn't manage to fall in love with any of the men she slept with.

When this finally happened, it was with a much older foreigner, married with five kids, who was temporarily living in Bulgaria. Hristina fell madly in love. He was fat, ugly, hairy, but also radiant and incredibly sweet. Hristina would melt whenever he smiled. His touch made her stomach flutter, and when they made love she was in seventh heaven. He was an apt and experienced lover.

Her brother found out about the foreigner almost immediately. He hadn't seen him in person, but was able to deduce his existence from the chaos in the apartment, where Hristina had never brought men before.

"What the hell are you doing, Sis?!" he whispered one night in their shared room when they happened to turn in at the same time.

"Shut up!"

"Are you bringing a buffalo in the apartment? My girlfriend's too grossed out to go there!"

"If you don't shut up, I'll slit your throat while you sleep!"

A few days later, Hristina moved into the other apartment. Her folks sensed that things were serious and didn't bother her about anything.

Hristina's romance lasted three months. Then, the foreigner returned to his country. For days on end, Hristina could feel his presence in the empty apartment. She heard his laugh and shivered at the memory of his touch. She spent hours in blissful reminiscence. One of the final nights, she'd asked her lover to go unprotected, and she was hoping she was pregnant.

One day, her brother came to see her at their parents' behest.

"How is it going, Sis? You good?" he asked.

"Never been better!" she replied, adding to herself, "Knock on wood!"

But fate had other plans. She got her period right on time. When she saw the trickling blood, Hristina burst into tears and cried all night. The following day, she no longer felt the presence of her lover around her. The apartment felt empty like a tomb. Hristina picked up her things and returned to the family one-bedroom. Her brother moved to the big apartment to give her space for her lovesickness.

In the daytime, Hristina went to work, and in the evenings she shut herself in her room. Her folks wondered what to do with her. Her mother would listen at Hristina's door.

"Hrissy, come have a bite," she beckoned.

The father started drinking alone in the kitchen at night, and the mother started nagging him. Things got tense. Only the granny kept her calm.

"She'll get over it," she kept on saying.

The first sign of change came when Hristina asked her father to trim the tree so she could watch the happenings on the street. Her father immediately obliged. He took out his ladder and started sawing the branches off.

While she was watching him work from her window, Hristina felt like crying, but she controlled the urge and just smiled and waved at him.

"I can lift your spirits!" he said in code, meaning he'd got a fresh bottle.

The two of them loved to drink Mastika.

When he heard his sister was feeling better, Ivan returned to the one-bedroom, and the Berovs were reunited once again. The two siblings continued to share the room of their childhood.

"You'll never get married, the two of you!" their mother nagged. "And it's all my fault!"

Hristina resumed watching the street life, perched by her window. Whenever she saw a gesture of intimacy between a man and a woman, she was overwhelmed with sadness. She remembered her foreigner. She remembered how fervently she had wished to conceive his child. At such moments, she'd step away from the window and go to the kitchen. There, she could find everything she needed to soothe her soul and fill up her empty days: love, Mastika and a salad of grilled peppers with red onions,olives and garlic.

After her affair with the foreigner, Hristina stopped dating. It was boring and pointless.

JOHNNY THE TIRE

Johnny graduated in engineering in his hometown, majoring in internal combustion engines. While Johnny was still in college his father, also an engineer, passed away. Thanks to his father's connections, Johnny's mother found him a job at a local plant, but Johnny turned the offer down.

"I'm a construction engineer, Mother! I'm not a mere implementer! I have ideas! If you start off as an implementer, you stay one for the rest of your life."

The mother took pride in the high goals her son had set for himself, but since she had given birth to him at a late age, she wanted Johnny to stand on his own two legs before she retired.

"You can accept the job and still pursue your dream."

"Do you happen to know who Bill Gates is?"

"Of course, I do."

"The man dropped out of Harvard to start his own business. Have you heard of Harvard?"

"Of course, I have, I'm not an idiot."

"Harvard! Mind you! Need I say more?"

Johnny was always well dressed. He was tidy, clean-shaven, and his hair was neatly trimmed. After graduating, he set out going about the city looking for sponsors. He was carrying a floppy disk, which he often waved in front of his mother and uncle.

"Check this out! A simple floppy disk! Do you know what's on it? You will soon learn!"

"Johnny," his uncle would try to bring him back down to earth, "what sponsors are you raving about, kiddo?! There are no sponsors in Bulgaria: sponsors live abroad."

"The right man in the right place can make all the difference, Uncle. Agreed?"

"Agreed, but..."

"Take a look! A mere floppy disk!"

Johnny kept this floppy disk in the pocket of his denim jacket as he went around hunting for sponsors.

"Do you know where our man is looking for sponsors?" his uncle once asked his mother. She instantly got scared out of her wits:

"Where?!"

"With the bookies."

"But he has no money on him! I give him one lev a day, and he won't even take it. He says, Mother, I don't need any cash: I don't smoke, I don't drink, I don't go out with girls..."

The same day, Johnny's mother tried to find out what business Johnny had with the soccer betting crowd.

"I'm after their money." Johnny said.

"Do you bet?"

"I don't."

"What then?"

"I advise the suckers who can't tell the difference between *Derby County* and *Ipswich Town*! What am I saying?! They don't so much as distinguish between *Wolverhampton* and *Southampton*, let alone the rest of the teams..."

"Do you make money on these consultations?"

"I don't. I only make contacts. Contacts matter more than money."

"I can't see how the bettors and your engineering project are related."

"The whole world is gambling, Mother. So are my potential sponsors. If there was an opera house in town, I would go to the opera, too. For networking's sake."

"If you know so much about it, why don't you bet yourself? Is it because you don't have money?"

"I do have money, what makes you think I don't? You give me one lev every day."

"Then why?"

"I aim high, Mother, how many times do I have to tell you that?"

"Tell me when you pick up a girlfriend, okay? I'll have to increase your daily allowance."

"If I pick up a girlfriend, Mother, she will give me a daily allowance, not you."

"Don't talk like that! Don't be stingy! Women don't like tight-fisted men."

"You are out of touch, Mother. Nowadays, men and women go Dutch: everyone pays their own bill.

Now and again, Johnny would pick up a girlfriend, but he didn't tell his mother. Few town girls could meet his high standards. Johnny dated girls mainly for the sake of his social contacts. In this way, he put to the test his social effectiveness. He used his contacts to take his girlfriends to a disco for free. He also took his dates to the theater for free, as he knew the people at the community center. Sometimes, he and his date would even get a free drink at a night club, as Johnny had tipped off the bartender which soccer team to bet on.

Johnny's practice as a consultant and a tipster extended to other activities. He started advising people what make car to buy, what sea-resort to go to, what to invest their money in, how to untie a complicated family tangle, or solve a love problem. The funny thing in this whole business was that he had neither a car, nor money, he didn't go to the seaside, he was not a family man, and he knew little about love.

Johnny had some inherent knowledge of life which he generously shared with his fellow citizens. He just knew things. He was ready with advice on any subject, and if nothing else, he managed to reassure those around him that there was always a solution to every problem.

People wondered why Johnny didn't bet and often asked him this question:

"You're trying to make money, right? Why don't you make bets?"

"You have no idea how much money I really need!"

"You can at least earn enough for your coffee…"

"Have you ever seen me drink coffee?"

"…or for a seaside vacation."

"My seaside vacation will be neither here, nor now: I'll go to an exotic island."

"Buy yourself a car then!"

"A car, or a wreck? I'll never buy a second-hand wreck, and money spent on a car is money thrown away: I need money for something else."

Johnny wouldn't be outtalked about anything.

Once, he met a woman who clung to him tight. She was older than him and tried to force him into marriage. Johnny tried to escape, but she wouldn't let go of him. One day, she panned him so hard that Johnny went speechless with amazement.

"You're afraid to live, man!" she raged. "You are always giving out advice, but you don't have a clue how to live your own life, neither do you have the guts to live it! You never take the leap for fear of failing! You don't want to buy a car, lest it turns out to be a wreck! You don't want to marry me! Look at me, just look at me! I am young, I have a good job, I earn good money, I am healthy, I'll give you children, you'll sponge off me for the rest of your life! What are you afraid of?"

Johnny gaped at his furious girlfriend with a keen interest. He had never seen such a dashing woman and had never heard someone advertise themselves in such a way. *"That's the spirit,"* he thought to himself, *"that's the way to sell!"* Despite the interest the girl managed to pique in him, he stopped seeing her, nevertheless.

"How's it going, find any sponsors?" his uncle joshed him from time to time.

"People who aim high achieve their goals with sweat on their brows. Don't think it was easy for Bill Gates. Do you know how long it took him to convince his sponsors to invest in him? Years!"

"Johnny, this is Bulgaria, kiddo! This is not America!"

"Do you think it's easy to make it in America? Do you think money grows on trees there? If you do, you're wrong! This is a popular fallacy. Success is harder to achieve in America than in Bulgaria. Need I say more?!"

Johnny's mother often shared her worries with her brother:

"He won't get a job, he won't get involved with a girl; I don't know what finding sponsors means, but I've already lost hope. I don't know what to scold him for. He doesn't smoke, he doesn't drink, he hardly eats. If I had a cat instead of a son, I would go to greater expense. He saves every lev I give him, buys new clothes and you see how well-dressed he always is: clean, tidy, a most wonderful boy!"

The years passed, yet Johnny never lost faith in his dream project. At first, people watched him with curiosity, then they gradually got tired of it all. Johnny continued waving about his floppy disk, which at one point became obsolete, as the new computers used CDs, not floppies. His mother retired, money was tight, so Johnny had to get a job. The industry in town collapsed, the plant, in which Johnny could have taken up a job as an engineer, shut down, and he had no alternative but to start work at a private warehouse.

By that time, the people in town had stopped taking Johnny seriously. They had nicknamed him Bill Gates. Due to an incident at the private warehouse, he got himself yet another nickname.

The owner of the warehouse needed his car tires changed for the winter, and he asked Johnny to do it. Johnny was shocked at this request, because as chief of the warehouse he organized his work in such a way as to avoid manual labor at all costs and never dirty his hands with anything: he kept record of all the stock, supervised the wholesale deals and filed the invoices, without doing any manual work whatsoever. He had a way with the customers. Johnny had them load up the purchased goods on the trucks themselves, and followed them around, cleanly dressed, advising them on everything: what to buy, when to buy it, how to load it, and so on. Johnny's employer reprimanded him and asked him to be more helpful with the customers, but then he realized that Johnny was an excellent salesman and stopped interfering. The customers left the warehouse grateful to Johnny and the trade went swimmingly.

So, one day, Johnny's employer asked him to change his car tires, and Johnny tried to find a man from a nearby warehouse to do the job. Everyone was busy, so, for the first time in his life, he got down to doing something with his own hands. A slushy November snow was falling and Johnny got wringing wet while he changed the tires.

Johnny's employer showed up two hours later and asked if his car was ready. When he saw it, he froze and face-palmed. Johnny had managed to somehow mount the tires the wrong side out.

　　　　　　　　　　　　　　　　　　　　

"Some job, man! How the hell did you manage that!?" his employer asked.

"It wasn't easy," Johnny replied.

"You bet! You've mounted the tires inside out! I thought you were an engineer?"

"A construction engineer."

"A construction engineer, I see..."

"Majored in internal combustion engines."

"You don't say!... Dear Lord! Oh, my God! Now I've seen it all!"

The employer, who on the whole thought highly of Johnny, spread the story of the tires around town. From then on, Johnny was demoted from *Bill Gates* to *Johnny the Tire*.

This foolish incident became folklore, and made Johnny a laughing stock. Even the betting crowd made fun of him and stopped asking him for advice. Otherwise, Johnny was still the same: he didn't touch alcohol, he didn't smoke, and he totally stopped going out with girls.

These stupid tires played yet another dirty trick on Johnny. The customers of the warehouse stopped listening to him. They wanted him to help them with the loading, not to jabber all the time, but since Johnny was mostly jabbering, the customers complained to his employer. He warned Johnny a couple of times, and eventually he fired him. Johnny got a job guarding a parking lot. He did shifts with two retirees.

After Bulgaria joined the European Union and Johnny learned that there would be European subsidies available, he went to the municipality to investigate how things worked. From the municipality he went straight to the cafe where the soccer bettors gathered and ordered a round of vodkas for everyone to celebrate the EU subsidies. For himself, he ordered a soda.

The soccer bettors asked:

"Hey, Johnny, do you still carry around that old floppy disk?"

"Yep."

"Let's have a look at it, you can't be serious!"

Johnny reached into the top pocket of his denim jacket and showed the floppy disk. This caused a storm of laughter in the cafe.

"Do reveal the secret, Johnny boy. Not the whole of it, just a tiny bit. Have mercy, give us a hint of what's on this floppy disk."

"Whatever is on it, will soon come to light. Need I say more?"

"Have a shot of vodka, Johnny. Otherwise, the European subsidies might pass you by."

"I'll have one, but not here and not now: somewhere else, for sure."

"Where? In the next world?"

"Maybe. This is yet to be seen."

"To Johnny! And to the European money!"

Johnny finished his soda, fished out a clean handkerchief, blew his nose in it, and secretly wiped away a tear.

Years passed.

Johnny put on weight. He continued to work as parking lot security guard. He was still neat, his clothes worn out with washing, hardly fitting him anymore. The town had long since forgotten about Johnny's floppy disk. Few remembered where his nickname, Johnny the Tire, had come from. People greeted him, but didn't notice him. They just didn't care about him. If he vanished into thin air, hardly would anyone know.

Johnny spent his free time with the betting crowd. He listened to them go on about soccer. He would sit alone at a table in the corner of the cafe. What was new about Johnny was he picked up the habit of drinking coffee. He drank it with a lot of sugar.

THE IMPORTANCE OF SMELLS

Sometimes Marusya had the feeling she was living two, or even three lives, instead of one. Her speed was supersonic. Marusya thought, talked and acted like a jet engine. To her, everyone seemed to think and talk slowly, yet she still differentiated between the slow and the really slow people. The really slow people got on her nerves. Whenever she had to deal with them, she took an anti-anxiety pill, which slowed her down considerably, but even so, she was still ten times faster than they were.

While talking to a really slow person, Marusya was also doing a bunch of other things: texting, fiddling with her meetings agenda, deciding on what to cook for dinner, recalling a scene from a film or a play she'd seen. Sometimes, enduring the pauses between the sentences of her interlocutors, Marusya fought the urge to do a quick run to the grocery store.

Marusya knew in advance what a really slow person was about to say.

"I understand!" she'd try to interrupt.

But this slowed down the conversation even further, as the snail usually started to wonder what exactly it was that Marusya understood, seeing as how he himself didn't know what he was about to say. Marusya had forbidden herself to say "I understand" but she couldn't help it. So, she usually followed it with "Sorry, go on."

Marusya weighed fifty kilos. She was the mother of a boy and a girl, aged twelve and nine. She had divorced their father and now she was living with her younger boyfriend. Marusya wanted to bear him a child, but she couldn't get pregnant. She was too skinny, the doctors said.

Marusya organized concerts and TV shows for singers and actors, birthday receptions for big shots, and she was a sought-after consultant for advertising, media and culture projects. She did the housework by herself. She cooked, looked after the kids, and always took the family on out-of-town weekend trips. She found time for everything, easily. Marusya was getting more efficient and sought-after in her work. She started turning down lower-paid projects, and thus she shot herself in the foot: she had even more spare time now.

"You're such a drama queen!" her best friend would say.

Marusya was like a bored cat, dying for something to happen.

And something did happen. For some time now, she'd been focusing on a certain person, the way a cat focuses on a faint, distant noise that may, or may not, be real.

The person had long legs, a nice bosom, a tiny bottom, a pretty face and she was no more than twenty. Marusya saw her at the office of the consulting agency, where her boyfriend worked. The girl was doing something, leaning over a desk. The boyfriend was at the other end of the room, talking to another guy, but his gaze was fixed on the girl. Marusya took a good look at her, and then forgot about her. But now those long legs came back to haunt her.

Direct as she was, Marusya announced her suspicions to all her friends.

"My Boyko has landed a young mistress!" she would say with a broad smile.

"You're imagining things," one of her acquaintances told her.

"I'm not imagining! Want to bet?"

They did.

"You're desperate for strong emotions," he said. "You're dependent on them like a junkie. You have to pull yourself together!"

Over the following months, Marusya lost another 5 kilos. Now she looked like an apparition. All that was left of her were her big, shiny eyes. Her best friend tried to convince Marusya that the mistress had nothing on her.

"You haven't even seen her," Marusya objected.

"I don't need to."

"She's very beautiful!"

"You're more beautiful."

"How do you know if you haven't seen her?"

"I don't have to see her, I can imagine her. You are a unique woman; chicks like her are a dime a dozen."

Wondering what to do, Marusya decided to have a child with her boyfriend and forced herself to eat more. While waiting for the really slow people to finish saying whatever they were saying, she was always munching on something.

Her boyfriend worked until late more and more often. He stopped joining her and the kids on their weekend trips outside the city. He grew silent and reticent. It often occurred to Marusya that her unspoken suspicions were driving him away, and that even if they were unfounded, she was going to lose him anyway. She knew she had to be more diligent with her feelings for him, but her suspicions always got the better of her, and she was passively watching her personal life fall apart.

She started having little cries in the bathroom. That didn't go unnoticed by her children. Her daughter would get easily upset with or without cause, and her son, who remembered the separation with his father, once said, "I'm sick of this!"

One evening, Marusya said to her boyfriend:

"We need to talk."

"Okay! I was going to say that, too," he replied.

After the kids were tucked in, the two of them sat down in the kitchen.

"Who goes first?" Marusya asked.

"I guess I should," he said. After a beat, he blurted out, "I love another woman. I'm sorry, we have to split up."

Marusya gaped at him, then she suddenly shouted:

"I knew it! It's the pretty girl in your office, right?"

"Yes."

"I knew it!" she shouted again with a broad smile.

Her boyfriend was confused.

"Don't mind me, I won a bet!" Marusya said.

The next day, her boyfriend moved out.

For the first week or so after the separation, Marusya was euphoric. Her suspicions hadn't been based on any facts, and yet they turned out to be true. She was supersonic indeed: she was quicker and more intuitive than fate itself.

Next, Marusya started bragging to everyone. She made her best friend eat crow over her inaccurate prediction regarding Marusya's uniqueness. She also called her acquaintance and said:

"I won the bet!"

But he didn't admit defeat so easily.

"That is yet to be seen. I have another hypothesis. It's a self-fulfilling prophecy. It was your suspicions that led to their affair, not the other way around."

Marusya knew that hard times were ahead of her, and she wanted to postpone them. She was a woman who couldn't hold on to a man. The recent developments were pretty much a repetition of what had happened with her ex-husband years before. Marusya dreaded the loneliness and the conclusion she would reach sooner or later: that she was a woman who couldn't hold on to a man.

"I'm in for a very bad crisis, just watch!" she warned her best friend, and started preparing for the crisis the way people prepare for a hurricane.

Time went by, the hurricane didn't hit, and Marusya began to wonder what was happening. She'd been sure she would resort to suicide, yet here she was, alive and kicking.

"I'm having an identity crisis," she said to her best friend. "I don't know who I am."

Marusya had just gone through a separation that was as trivial, vulgar and stupid as a soap opera, and yet she wasn't suffering.

One day, while she was packing up the last of her ex-boyfriend's things with the intention to give them back to him, Marusya paused at a bottle of cologne he used to wear. She sprayed some on her wrist, took a sniff at it and suddenly realized that she didn't love the owner of that cologne. She had never loved him. She had hooked up with him just to show her ex-husband that younger men found her attractive.

Marusya sniffed at the cologne again,

"Of course!" she said and rang her best friend up. "I'm so happy, you can't imagine! Poor Hacho! I did something horrible to him! I used him, then pushed him into the arms of that girl! I hope he's happy with her!"

For some time afterwards, Marusya was telling everyone about the enormous importance of smells in a person's life.

"There's nothing more important! If I hadn't smelled that cologne, I would have killed myself and orphaned my children. Good thing I smelled it! I was willing to have another child, just

to keep a man I felt nothing for! We underestimate the significance of smells in our lives. It may well be more important than
the significance of the mind."

FIVE KIDS AND FIVE DOGS

"Try the phyllo pie, sister. I hadn't made one in a while, but this one turned out a beauty, taste it, it's delicious. The kids are gobbling it up... My, they are starving to death in that home, sister, I'm telling you! The caregivers, are decent people, though. The papers say otherwise, but the women at this institution are alright. Thing is, when money's tight, how can you feed all these children, eh?! If I told you what food they give them, you wouldn't believe it... Hey, Milla, why are you rummaging in there, sweetie?! Don't do that, my girl, go play on the computer with the other kids!... This Milla girl, she pilfers the most! Watch her now, just watch her! She keeps her eyes peeled at all times, and she'll rob me in the end, you can bet on it. It runs in their blood, you know. Shocking, isn't it? I myself was shocked in the beginning. You open your home up to them, you feed them, you give them presents; they thank me, they hug me and kiss me, we dance together and when they are gone, I find out they've robbed me! The first time around, they had a go at my purse and stole my cash. All of it! They even took the small change! I was shocked, just like you. Mostly because of the small change, I guess. I took it to heart, and I thought to myself, *"Okay, that's that, I won't be able to stick it out with them."* But here I am, I made it!... This wretched Milla!... Hey, Milla, didn't you hear me, sweetie?! Go play on the computer with the other kids!... You liked my phyllo pie?... Let's drink some red wine, sister, shall we? We haven't seen each other in ages!... Don't think of me as a Mother Teresa: my taking care of them, buying them things and teaching them computer literacy is paid for. There's this European program for abandoned children. I even took them on a trip: boy, was that a comedy of errors!... Oh, dear!... I'll tell you about it some other time! There wasn't a living soul around who didn't get burned. And who do you think bore the shame and covered all the damages in the end? Me, of course. It was quite a lark!... How far did you get, kids? Good job, Hristo! Now, give your seat to Lily. Lily, sit down, sweetie! Don't pull back, there's nothing to be afraid of! Hristo, give Lily a hand!... Lily's afraid that she might break the computer. Look at her, she won't touch it. She must have been beaten as a child for some mischief and was probably traumatized. Now,... try not to get shocked again... It was she who stole a silver ring from me. You know me, I don't wear bling, but I bought this one when I was young and I could still pass for a dish. So, Lily found it, took it and since she's a little kid, she held it in her fist and hid her fist behind her back. She did!... After they robbed me the first time, I gave them such a lecture that I almost made myself cry. I talked to them, I went right for their heartstrings, the girls and the youngest one here, Goshko, they all cried: Goshko started to hiccup, and I couldn't calm him down. Then, when they left, I found out that the bowl in which I had put fruit for them was gone: it was made of metal and therefore good to sell for scrap. Well?! Ha-ha-ha... What do you say to that?!... Dino, stop it, baby! Dino's in heat again!... Truth is, sister, these dogs are a bit too much, but what can I do when they just cling to me! At the moment, I don't even know if there are five, or six of them. Don't laugh, I really don't. Silly me! Thing is, the most recent one I took in, the Prime Minister, sometimes spends the night outside. I don't think I've seen him today. Dino is short for "dinosaur", look how ugly he is. Ever seen an uglier dog? You can see he's scabby now and he's always in heat. Ugly, scabby and horny. I've tried every ointment there is! You can probably smell his stench... well, this now is nothing – you should come see when I've just applied the ointment – you won't stand the stench! I open all the windows, and still! These scabs just won't heal! At some point, I felt I couldn't stand it anymore. *"I'll get rid of Dino,"* I told myself, *"no matter what!"* Well, it's not so easy to get rid of a dog you've had since it was a puppy! Not easy at all. For a whole month, I made mental preparations. One night, I took him out and walked him around the neighborhood. I kept going further and further away from our building. Why I was doing it, I didn't know. While we were walking, Dino, who is otherwise cowardly and vicious (he has bitten me twice on the hand. "A dog that bites the hand that feeds it, must be chased away immediately," this is what old dog-owners say)... So, that night, Dino unexpectedly made friends with a few stray dogs, he started playing with them, and I turned back and walked away slowly and quietly. There must have been a bitch in heat among these dogs. I can't tell you what I felt while I was walking away from that place, sister! I thought to myself, *"Now he'll find out I'm leaving him behind and he'll run after me."* I walked without looking back. I walked one block away, then another one, and only then did I turn to take a look: the street was empty and deserted! I wanted to cry out with joy and relief. *"It's over,"* I said to myself, *"I won't see this scabby dog anymore!"* I felt like singing! I approached our building and just before entering it, I heard the sound of claws on the asphalt behind me. I will never forget that sound! The sound of claws scratching on the asphalt – a terrible sound! I felt like crying! Dino clung to me as if nothing had happened and we got back home together... Dino, Dino, get off Mutza's back, buddy! Mutza, go on, git!... I don't even want to think about what I'm gonna do with all the new-born puppies.

                                   LUDMIL TODOROV

Don't think being ugly and scabby is an obstacle: God knows how many puppies Dino has fathered. Let's drink, sister, you're not drinking much, only I am and I'll certainly get drunk!... Well, well, the Prime Minister's here! Where have you been, Prime Minister? Huh? What have you been up to? He wants to play! He wants to play all the time! And he is always trying to kiss you on the mouth. My big kisser!... Look at Milla! Oh, boy! Her mind is set on snatching something, but she doesn't know what! I bet she'll filch something stupid, I just pray they don't start stealing books: some of my books are priceless, you know! But I don't think they'll do that. When I see them off, I give them a quick frisk, just to check for books. They also steal clothes from me. Oh, boy, check out our Milla here! She's so funny! Hey, Milla, what are you up to, girl?! Go play on the computer, now!... Toshko, what is it you want?... The Coca Cola's in the fridge, go bring it and pour some for the other kids, too. OK? Don't drink it all by yourself! If you drink it all by yourself, I'll be angry with you!... Sometimes, I can't stand it anymore, sister! I'm not talking about the kids and the dogs. It's just... how shall I put it... sometimes I have the feeling that this guy up there has singled me out to conduct an experiment with me. You know me, I'm not the grumbling kind. I'm not talking about my circumstances. Not even about being alone and childless. There are many women like me, what can you do, fate has willed it that way. No one's to blame, it's just the way my life's turned out. But sometimes I really get the feeling that someone is experimenting with me. Don't worry, I'm not crazy, just fumbling for the right words. The trials I have to endure seem to be well-ordered, somehow intended. Not a single moment passes by without me going through some trial. Sometimes, it's about some stupid crap. I have the feeling that whoever sends it out to me has run out of ideas and since they can't think of a good ordeal, they send me all sorts of crap, just to keep me busy. A few months ago, I got a phone bill for two thousand leva. Can you imagine that?! My bills almost never exceed thirty leva, mind you. Just an example. And within the past two years, I had the front door replaced three times, and you know why? I lock the door when I go out and when I return, the lock gets stuck, the door won't open, and I can't get in. I call a locksmith, he breaks the lock, and – you know how doors are nowadays – if you break the lock, you're better off buying a new door. Three times it happened! I can go on and on about it: it's a long list of mishaps that hit me on a daily basis! And that's just the stupid stuff! I don't even want to mention the really bad stuff: my best friend was in a coma for three years. Meanwhile, my mother got sick. When Mom passed away, a cousin of mine cheated me and misappropriated my share of the family inheritance. By the way, the family inheritance was not small: there was land that may be worth millions today. You know me, I'm a gullible person, but believe me, it's not out of stupidity: I constantly lose important files on my computer, even though I'm good with computers. Let me tell you about an incident that happened to me, and you'll get the picture. Care for some more wine? You don't, fine!... Once, I took them all on a trip to the countryside. All of them, the whole menagerie you see here. Except for the Prime Minister. Five kids and five dogs! We all jammed into my tiny Ford Fiesta. A loyal car, freshly repaired! We set off a bit late: we didn't leave until noon, instead of early in the morning. I got a flat tire, but I had a spare one and I changed it. I got a second flat tire: this time a truck driver gave me a hand and glued it for me. I got yet a third flat tire... it sounds ridiculous, I know! That reminds me of a hunter joke: A hunter was once telling a tall tale about a bear in the woods, popping up in front of him; then, another bear popped up behind his back; a third one appeared on his left and yet a fourth one appeared on his right. When his amused listeners asked him what had happened in the end, he replied, "They ate me!"... My case exactly! There came a good stranger and glued my third flat tire for me. By that time, it had started getting late: it was late autumn, in November. So, there I was, driving, more dead than alive. It was getting dark. And then I thought to myself, *"If I get another flat tire, at least I will know for sure that someone is conducting an experiment with me."* I didn't get a flat, but guess what! The engine of my newly repaired car blew up. So, there I was left on the road, in the middle of the night, with five kids and five dogs. You know what, since then, I have been haunted by an irrational feeling that someone is testing me, checking how much longer I can endure and whether I will not change after all this, whether I will not give up the dogs, the kids, and everything I believe in. Whether I will not become embittered, whether I will not hate, reject, curse, cross out, stop believing – not in God, I'm not a believer – but in people, in life, in, I don't know what, you get the gist! After this incident, I started feeling not like a target or a victim, but like a warrior, like a fighter defending some borders. I call them *borders of humanity*. And I said to myself, *"Okay, I see, I am expected to endure, nothing more! Great, fine! I'm good at that!"*... Drink, sister, I've had my fill!... Hey, kids, you wanna dance?... Okay, hold on!... I play Viennese waltzes for them. At first, they were stupefied and they giggled because they were used to pop folk and belly-dances. Now you just watch them belly-dancing to Strauss! They got accustomed to his music. I've set out to cleanse their minds a bit, or else God knows when they will listen to Strauss's works!... Oh, no!... Oh, boy!... They've stolen my wallet!... Shoot, when did they?! I deliberately put it in my cardigan pocket and I never took my hand out of it! But there we are!... So, see? The experiment is still on! But I don't give up easily!... Hey, kids, kids, hold it!... One of you has stolen my wallet! Don't make me search you! I don't want to search you: it's humiliating! Now I'm gonna play the music again, you go on dancing and whoever has taken my wallet, must find a way... without being noticed by anyone... to drop it on the floor! Am I clear?... Okay, let's get going!... Strauss! Strauss alone can straighten things out for them! I'll drive them mad with Strauss, so, hopefully, they might forget about stealing!"

ON VACATION

Galya and Milen Popov used to go on vacation to Greece, but after the upheavals there, they decided to change destinations and go to Italy, instead. They did their research, hopped into their brand new Audi and hit the road, through Serbia. Their daughter lived in Slovenia, but they didn't drop by to see her because... well, because they were in the mood for vacation, not for family reunions. Their daughter was married to a Slovenian journalist. She had given birth to a boy two years ago, but they'd only seen him on the Internet.

Galya and Milen Popov worked in the finance sector. They were self-made and knew the value of money. For Bulgarian standards, they were a wealthy family. They could afford a trip not only to Greece or Italy, but to Acapulco and Honolulu. Yet, they didn't indulge themselves. The Popovs went for much more humble resorts than most wealthy Bulgarians, and unlike them, didn't stay at expensive hotels, but always settled for inexpensive house rentals. Not the cheapest, but cheap enough for them to take pleasure in the deal. The perfect vacation rental had to have a barbecue, or at least a yard where the Popovs could set up their own barbecue, so they didn't have to eat out. To go to the seaside without your own barbecue is like going without a beach umbrella: you incur extra expenses.

Galya and Milen Popov were beautiful, rich, well-groomed middle-aged people. And while they were cheap about umbrellas and restaurants, they drove a brand new Audi worth a hundred thousand euro.

"How come!?" those of you who know nothing about finances would ask.

Let me tell you how! A poor man has no way of knowing that if you save on umbrellas and pubs, you drive a new Audi, but if you spend on umbrellas and pubs, you drive a wreck. This is a complicated topic, and we'll leave it at that.

So, the Popovs crossed Slovenia without calling their daughter and went on vacation in a small Italian town. Galya Popov had no desire to see her grandson just now. The thought that she was someone's grandmother brought on negative emotions that she wanted to avoid during her summer trip. Galya read books on relaxation, followed special diets and sometimes did yoga, and she couldn't let her efforts be undone by some two-year-old snot. She had enough on her mind, she didn't need negative emotions during her annual vacation.

Contrary to their habit, the Popovs left Bulgaria without booking a rental house, relying on low demand during the global economic crisis. However, it turned out that all rental houses in town were occupied, so the Popovs were forced to spend the night in a hotel. It was small, filthy and cheap, but a hotel nevertheless.

Their mood darkened.

If you're rubbing your hands in anticipation of a drama, you'll be disappointed. Galya and Milen Popov were an examplary close-knit couple. They helped each other and never lied or cheated on each other. After the night at the hotel, they found a guest house that had no AC, true, but it had a small yard, where they set up their own barbecue. They filled up the fridge with food, and so their vacation began.

　　　　　　　　　　　　　　　LUDMIL TODOROV

They went to beaches far away from town, and they didn't pay either for umbrellas or parking, nor wasted any money on soda and ice cream.

On the beach, they collected shells and pebbles. Galya had a soft spot for the mineral world. Their house in Bulgaria was full of the mineral world.

The afternoons in the house were slightly unpleasant, what with the lack of AC, but the Popovs had developed a simple defense mechanism that protected them from emotional – shall we call it – discomfort. The mechanism went as follows: we have no AC, true, and it's hot as hell, and we're sweating like slaves, but are we saving money? We are! That's what counts!

That thought technique seemed like a loan from one of the eastern religions that teach you how to be happy even while you're being roasted on a spit. Joking aside, if the difficulties the Popovs were having brought even a minimal profit, the couple was happy.

Happiness has a price, and Galya Popov was gladly paying it by buying an excess of unnecessary clothes that overwhelmed her house as much as her pebbles and shells. After browsing long and strenuously in the commercial streets of the resorts they visited, Galya always bought a ton of junk, just because she had found it at ridiculously low prices.

But again, what is the point of saving on umbrellas and AC, if you squander it on junk? The answer is simple. When an expense brings joy, it is necessary and justified. Spending on umbrellas and AC does not bring joy, it merely brings relief. If you brace yourself, the sun sets and you stop sweating, while buying clothes, as long as they are cheap, brings 100-percent joy.

While Galya Popov was scavenging the streets of the little Italian town, Milen Popov was looking for happiness in his own peculiar way. Since their rental house had no Internet connection, and as the service was still expensive back in those days, he was hunting for an unprotected Wi-Fi router of a hotel or office, via which he could access the Internet totally free of charge.

Now! We must pay attention, because here things get a little weird. To be a rich man like Milen Popov searching for free Wi-Fi in a small Italian town is not what it seems. To a millionaire, petty theft is a sophisticated experience, not a pathological condition. Milen felt like a carefree youngster, rather than like Shylock.

The Popovs' vacation in the small Italian town was going swimmingly, until one sunny day, on the street, they ran into a couple of acquaintances from Bulgaria.

"Where on Earth do we have to go to avoid Bulgarians?!" Galya was fuming later, after they had agreed to go to a restaurant with the other family. And not just any restaurant, but an expensive one.

"I don't understand it," Milen commented. "Why are Balkan people so eager to spend money they don't have? Take the Greeks – they've gone bankrupt!"

Milen hated losing negotiations, and now he was mad that the intruders had managed to trick them into eating out.

"Did you see their car?" he asked.

"Don't get me started!"

"How the hell can you drive such a crappy car and sleep in a hotel at the same time?! What's more, you even eat at the hotel restaurant! Where is this going to lead us?! And by "us", I mean the whole of Europe!"

"To the bitter end," Galya replied, already thinking about her evening outfit, and not so much about Europe.

As soon as they were seated at the restaurant, the Popovs announced they were not hungry and would only order salads, maybe dessert, but that would be all. Also, they'd only drink

　　　　　　　　　　　　　　　LUDMIL TODOROV

mineral water. Indeed, the Popovs weren't hungry: before leaving for the restaurant, they had grilled some meat on their barbecue and dined at home.

Yes, but when someone is reckless, they don't take a hint. The other family ordered on and on. They had salads, appetizers, main courses, wine, desserts. They ordered a second bottle of wine. And to top it all – a cheeses plate to go with it, which made the Popovs exchange glances. The intruders nearly ordered digestifs, too. They got drunk and insisted on paying the bill, but Milen didn't agree, so the two families paid separately.

"Why didn't you let them pay for dinner?" Galya asked later, even though she knew the answer.

"If you allow someone to buy you dinner, sooner or later they'll want something in return."

"Yes, indeed."

The Popovs treated the intruders with measured indifference, hoping that would be their first and only get-together, but they were wrong. On the very next day, the man phoned Milen to say he'd done some research and had found the best restaurant in town.

Milen got the call in the morning while he and Galya were at the beach. It was depressing that from now on they had to dance to the tune of people they barely knew. The Popovs slumped under their umbrella like shipwreck survivors.

Suddenly, Milen said:

"What the hell! Let's live for once!"

This was the first fundamental, but really fundamental and pivotal divergence in the Popovs' married life.

Galya looked at her husband, horrified.

"Let's live for once?! What do you mean?!"

"Let's loosen the purse strings! We'll start spending along with them, and we'll see how long they can keep up!"

Galya couldn't understand what Milen was saying to her.

"I cannot fathom you, Milen! For the first time since we've been together, I cannot understand you! For real!"

"Okay then, you've got a better idea?"

"Of course I do! We can't let them force their model on us!"

"That ship has sailed!"

"We don't have to play their game!"

"I promised we'd be there. They'll wait for us in front of the hotel."

"Which hotel?"

"Oh my god!" Milen said, head in hands. "Last night they asked where we were staying, and I couldn't tell them we're renting a house, so I said we're at Hotel Corleone."

The expression of horror returned to Galya's face.

"What's this Hotel Corleone?"

"It's the fancy one, on the cliffs."

Galya took this in and shut up. She thought for a while. Then she said:

"We won't pick up our phones."

"They'll ask at the front desk, and they'll know we never registered there."

"Okay, what then?"

"Like I said, we'll start spending money alongside them, and I promise you, they'll go broke in no time."

"No way! Just forget it! This is madness!"

"Do we have any options?"

Galya's brain was racing.

"We'll meet them and we'll put an end to this!" she said. "We'll tell them we want to spend our vacation by ourselves."

"Alright, but we should move into Hotel Corleone for a while, just to be sure."

"What? Why!?"

"Because sooner or later they'll try to find us there for some nonsense..."

"What nonsense!?"

"Sundaes, for example!"

"Sundays!?"

"Yes!"

"What!?"

"They'll ask us out for sundaes."

"I can't understand what you're saying to me, Milen!"

"I'm giving you an example! They are a pesky couple, they'll drop by unannounced."

"What do we care?"

"They won't find us in the register!"

"So?"

"They'll tell everyone back home that we're liars. We can't afford that. We are financial experts with a reputation. We have to either move to Hotel Corleone, or..."

"Or what?"

"We can go see our grandson."

"No way, forget it!" Galya said and started pacing to and fro on the shore. "I'm not going! I don't want to feel like a grandmother while I'm supposed to be relaxing! It's out of the question! We have to go see him eventually, but why now? We got his pictures, we sent him gifts... We can send money, if needed. But I just hate this stupid Slavic custom!... What? Why should I go visit a child I feel nothing for? Why should I act the grandmother if I'm not feeling like one? I'll be a grandmother when I'm old! But right now, it's out of the question!"

Galya stopped pacing and looked into the horizon. She turned around and said:

"Okay, can't we just tell them we're unhappy with Hotel Corleone and we're checking out? Then we can explain that we'd like to spend our vacation by ourselves."

Milen processed this and said:

"It's an option."

So, that's what they did. In the evening, their acquaintances took them to a cheap pub, which proved Milen's hypothesis that they could not last long financially, and the two couples parted ways, wishing each other a nice vacation.

The next day, the Popovs started feeling blissful again. In the mornings they gathered minerals and shells on the beach, in the afternoons they were happily sweating in their room without AC, and in the evenings she went shopping, and he went hunting for free Wi-Fi.

Soon, they forgot all about the unpleasant incident with the intruders. Just one little thing was still bugging them, but they avoided the subject: the bill they had paid in the fancy restaurant.

A few days later, Galya said to Milen:

"Don't worry about that bill, I made up for it."

"How?"

"I sold some of the clothes I bought, at a profit."

"You did!? Where?"

"At the flea market."

"You're a genius!"

Nothing else darkened the Popovs' vacation in the small Italian town. They got tanned, filled the Audi with stones and headed back to Bulgaria.

We already mentioned how close-knit a couple the Popovs were. They could read each other's minds at any given moment, so when they entered Slovenia, both of them fell silent.

"We'll reach the exit soon," Milen sighed.

"Alright. Pull over, we need to think."

Milen pulled over in the shoulder lane. Galya got out of the car and started pacing to and fro, hands behind her back. She looked like a general on the eve of a major battle. Suddenly, she squatted, took a stone from the road, inspected it and brought it back to Milen in the car.

"Milen, I'm not ready to be a grandmother. We can visit the kids another time. It's only a few hours' drive... Look at this stone I found!" she said happily and showed the stone to Milen.

It was an ordinary round stone. Milen had given up appreciating the value of Galya's findings.

They got into the Audi and drove on toBulgaria.

Galya was smiling in the shotgun seat. She caressed the round stone in her hands, and soon it warmed up like a baby's bottom.

CRICKET

Old Maria lived alone in her apartment in her native town. Her younger son lived in the same town, and the elder one lived in the capital. Her husband had died twenty years earlier. Old Maria's apartment was in the town center, and whenever she was out on her front balcony, she felt as if she was out on the "main drag" where socializing and courting used to take place in her youth.

Old Maria had suffered a serious stroke, and that was consuming all of her time and attention. Her sons took good care of her, and only loneliness tormented her, but Old Maria preferred to be on her own and out of their way. She hoped she was not long for this world. Life is difficult after a stroke.

Lonely people notice things that others don't. In the summer, a cricket entered into Old Maria's life. It was singing in the branches of the walnut tree behind the building. The homeowners had planted the tree when they first moved in. For the first twenty years no one thought the tree would grow, it was puny and they even considered felling it at one point. But then it suddenly bulked up and embraced the building. The thick shade of its crown protected the rear balconies from the sun.

Old Maria's downstairs neighbor complained that the walnut's shade was too thick. A conflict ensued between the two old ladies. The neighbor hired a man with a chainsaw to cut off a big branch of the tree.

Back then, Old Maria was still in good health, and as soon as she heard the buzz of the chainsaw, she ran out onto her balcony and started convincing the man to stop cutting, as cutting down and mutilating trees was against the law. Her neighbor chimed in by saying that it was people like Old Maria, who ought to be outlawed for meddling in other people's lives. The quarrel between the two old ladies scared off the man with the chainsaw, and he climbed down the tree.

Next, the neighbor poured a can of gas over the walnut's roots. The two old ladies awaited the result anxiously. There was no result. The neighbor got ambitious and one day Old Maria saw her perching on the walnut tree with a small axe in her hand.

"Nikolina, come down!" Old Maria shouted.

"No! I want to fall down and weigh on your conscience!"

"Nikolina, come down, I'll call the guy to trim it!"

"No, you won't! You're just trying to trick me, but I'm not coming down! I'll weigh on your conscience!"

The neighbor started hacking at the branch that was marked by the chainsaw. She managed to chop off some of the bark, and that was that.

The cricket settled in the walnut tree in the summer. Every night it sang to Old Maria. The TV was always showing the same nonsense, so Old Maria would turn it off and enjoy the song of the cricket. She thought of her youth, of a life that went by as if in a blink, she revived old memories.

In the morning, she would go out and sit on a bench in front of the building, together with two men who also had suffered strokes. They were kind old gentlemen with small pensions. Thanks to her caring sons, Old Maria sometimes felt like a wealthy woman and treated them to coffee and ice cream.

One day, she bragged to her friends about her new neighbor.

"I have a little pal! Very vocal! It sings to me every night!"

After an entire week of unceasing nightly serenades, Old Maria felt drained of her energy. To say that crickets actually *sing* is inaccurate. Crickets don't sing, they *scrape*. Old Maria learned that the hard way. Her little pal wouldn't let her sleep.

Two sleepless nights later, she complained to her friends, and they said the cricket had probably relocated, and was now singing – correction: *scraping* – in a flower pot on her balcony.

Old Maria shook a broom at the flowers, but the cricket *sang* all night, nevertheless.

"Do you close the balcony door at night?" her friends asked.

"No, it's too hot."

"Leave another door open, and close the balcony!"

Old Maria followed the advice, but there was no improvement.

"It must be in the room!" one of the gentlemen concluded.

"You can't know for sure," the other one said. "Old people hear certain frequencies better than the young. I can hardly hear you, but if there's a termite around, I'll hear it immediately. A question of frequencies."

Old Maria started going to sleep with the TV on. She'd wake up with a headache in the middle of the night, turn the TV off and listen to the cricket scrape until morning.

People who have suffered a stroke get tired faster and need more sleep. What had started as a joke turned into a real problem, as the cricket upset Old Maria's delicate balance and disrupted her entire routine. She started sleeping during the day and spent her nights staring in the dark. She felt weak, feeble, haunted by old-age fears for her sons and their families.

There comes a time in old people's lives when they become weaker than a cricket, but try explaining that to the young. Old Maria complained to her younger son, and he said:

"So, what do you want from me? To protect you from a cricket?"

Yes, that was exactly what she wanted!

"Brother called me specially to ask about your cricket. What's with the cricket, he says, that's all Mom talks about. Let's give your tyrant a name, how about it?"

Old Maria laughed, but then she cried, because it was both funny and sad.

One day her son bought a can of Raid. He sent his mother out for a walk and sprayed everywhere, including the flower pots on the balcony and the nearest branches of the walnut tree.

When it got dark, Old Maria started waiting for the result. The evening news on TV was over, the series began, but the cricket was silent. At the end of the series she heard it again: loud and clear, as if it was right next to her. Suddenly, she realized that the cricket was behind the sofa. She sprayed some Raid there and the cricket went mute.

Old Maria slept soundly all night, and on the next day she told her friends through tears about her misadventure.

"I killed it! I killed my little pal that used to sing to me at night!"

"It didn't sing, it scraped!" her amused listeners corrected her.

Old Maria treated them to coffee and ice cream. In her mind, she was holding a wake for the cricket.

From that day on, the cricket moved into Old Maria's head. The thought that she'd killed an innocent creature gave her no peace. At night, she suffered pangs of remorse that she'd never felt before. People have no time for remorse: they must live, labor, raise kids, but now life had burdened her with the guilt of killing a cricket, and she could hardly sleep at night. The silence in the room seemed to accuse her. Old Maria had been long prepared for death. Now she wished for it even harder, but death doesn't come on a wish, it is God's work.

Old Maria went to church on holidays, accompanied by a friend of hers, but now she decided to go alone.

It was a difficult journey. After the stroke, Old Maria could hardly walk. Her left arm was paralyzed, and her left foot dragged on the ground. A set of stairs without a railing was the most taxing part. While climbing up them, she almost lost her balance, but luckily there was a young man nearby, who caught her.

Inside the church, Old Maria lit candles for her parents, her husband and the cricket. She prayed to God to forgive her this mortal sin. She got overemotional, she wept. Then she somehow returned home and slept all day from exhaustion.

In the evening, just before the TV series was over, the cricket sang again.

It was singing in the walnut tree. Old Maria was overwhelmed. She managed to kneel on the floor and started crossing herself, grateful for the mercy she was shown at that difficult moment.

The next day, her son found her dead on the floor: small, leaning on one side, her calm, relaxed face no longer marked by suffering and pain.

THE ENCOUNTER

Spring came and all the little critters in the city got moving. They started whistling, flitting about, mewing, tweeting, hopping, dragging after one another like lovesick fools, and Mima didn't know where to look and who to worry about first.

In the morning, while she was waiting for the trolleybus, a rat appeared on the boulevard and all the cars rushed at it. Tires squeaked inches away from its whiskers, and it was paralyzed with fear and dared not move.

Mima stood on the sidewalk, gaping. The rat was horror-stricken, and that was saving its life. If it tried to escape, it would be run over in an instant.

The traffic lights turned red, all automobiles stopped, and Mima stepped down onto the street.

"Shoo! Shoo! Go on, git!"

The rat didn't move.

Traffic resumed, Mima returned to the sidewalk. A car ran over the rat's whiskers. The rat did not stir.

As soon as the traffic lights turned red again, Mima stepped onto the street and lightly kicked the rat toward the curb. It rolled over once and lay on its back. At the sight of its pink belly, Mima felt sick. It was a female rat: a doe with tits. It lay exactly where the right-side tires of the cars would pass.

The traffic lights turned yellow and Mima panicked. She took a deep breath, grabbed the rat – the she-rat, to be precise –

and threw her onto the sidewalk. The animal dropped on its side as if it was dead.

Mima leaned over it. The she-rat was breathing fast. After a while, she raised her head and started sniffing around. Her whiskers twitched, she got to her feet and dragged herself towards the nearest apartment building.

Mima escorted her to protect her from the pedestrians.

The rat entered the building, and Mima stayed outside, helplessly looking around. She wasn't sure if she had accomplished her mission.

Mima was a journalist and hosted a cultural talk-show at a radio station whose studio was located in a large park. As she walked through the park, she looked around to see some bird in the trees, so she could unload the stress of rescuing the she-rat. The trees were still bare, but the green was somehow implied. Mima loved this stage of spring the most, when the green is implied.

Shortly before she reached the building where the radio studio was, she spotted a blackbird.

A blackbird is hard to stalk. This one was obviously starving, and Mima saw it up close sitting by a trash can. The blackbird got startled and flew off. Mima stopped by the trash can and stared in amazement. The eyes of the blackbird were blue.

So blackbirds have blue eyes! Who knew!

This discovery fascinated Mima, and she remained by the trash can, looking at the bird that had perched on a twig, waiting for the intruder to scram.

"Well, how on earth can they be blue?!" she exclaimed, while the blackbird looked away in an entirely different direction. It acted as if it had little interest in the garbage.

Mima decided to test its patience and froze in her spot. She noticed the blackbird was putting on airs. Its blue eyes darted down to the garbage, though, and Mima's smile got broader and broader.

"Aren't we special!"

The blackbird's blue eyes enchanted Mima, and she went on to the studio amused.

Mima's husband passed away the winter before. He died quite young, not yet forty. After sending him off from this world, Mima went to the seaside resort where the two of them had met. She checked into an empty, cold hotel with the intention of revisiting the places of their first dates. Alas, the icy wind wouldn't let her walk to the seashore.

The next day she left the seaside town and went to visit a friend of hers from college. Her friend lamented her so hard that Mima left her place in a hurry. Her next stop was with former high school classmates, a family of doctors. Doctors encounter death every day and are not easily shocked by it. That suited Mima, and she stayed with them a bit longer.

After this journey, Mima returned to Sofia, her grief overcome. The ease with which this had happened puzzled her friends. They wondered if there was a new man in Mima's life. After all, she was thirty-seven. Mima took in this unspoken question with a smile. She believed in the immortality of the soul, and she thought it wrong to mourn a person whose soul was still available, so to speak. She loved her late husband and their 15-year-old son dearly, and her attachment to animals was proverbial. Instead of going on about her loss, she would talk about her beloved pet cat named after the great violinist Yehudi Menuhin, or admire the intelligence of crows and the stupidity of sparrows, and as of late, her new crush were sheep: she called them "baby dolls" and all sorts of terms of endearment.

On the day in question, Mima bored a colleague of hers with the story of saving the rat and he scolded her:

"Mima, enough of this rat-talk, sweetheart!"

Mima's show aired in the afternoon, so she took some time to go feed a stray cat that lived in front of the building's entrance. Sometimes stray dogs gathered there, too. The cat was not afraid of anything, it was Mima who was afraid for the cat, running downstairs every other hour to check if the cat was safe. That even happened once while the show was on the air: during a music break, Mima noticed a pack of stray dogs surrounding the cat, she opened the studio window, and shouted at them menacingly. The dogs raised their heads to look at her, and the cat escaped.

That day Mima had invited a famous elderly actor on her talk-show. The two of them had known each other for years and when the actor arrived, Mima began telling him about the rat.

The guest listened to her intently, absorbing every bit of the story. The two sat in front of the microphones at the very last minute, and the show began somewhat aimlessly and scattered.

Asked by the presenter about the challenges of his profession, the actor told her about some incident and ended the story with:

"I felt just like that rat you told me about... Or was it a she-rat?" he asked Mima.

"A she-rat, yes..."

"I felt just like that she-rat of yours... But then, our listeners don't know what we are talking about. Tell them in a few words, please."

"We'd better talk about you..."

"Well, telling them about the she-rat, is the same as if we're talking about me."

A rule of thumb in journalism is that presenters never talk about themselves. Mima knew it very well, but the actor asked her quite persistently, and she couldn't help telling the story of

　　　　　　　　　　LUDMIL TODOROV

that morning. From then on the show became so idiotic that when it was over, her boss called her to his office.

"This man is one of Bulgaria's most beloved actors and instead of letting him talk about himself, you told the listeners about some rat!"

"I apologize. I'm terribly sorry!"

"Mima, I know it's not easy for you, darling, but we can't go on like this! You rescue cats during the show, and now you tell the listeners how you rescued a rat. Do you need some time off? I can give you leave without pay."

"No, thanks, I'm terribly sorry, it won't happen again."

"I certainly hope so."

"Promise! I swear! Never again!"

Mima knew that if she made another mistake, her boss would fire her.

On her way home from work, she was overcome with uneasy thoughts and sat down on a park bench. She had to pull herself together, or she would lose her job. She hadn't felt so bad in a long time. She felt like crying.

At some point, a man and a dog passed by. The dog was on a leash. It looked Mima deep in the eyes and stopped. Its master pulled, but the dog wouldn't budge. The man loosened the leash, and the dog walked over to Mima, so the man tugged it back again.

The dog resisted with all the weight of its substantial body. The man gave it a tug, but it refused to move, so the man finally began to drag it.

Mima waited for the dog to give up, but it kept pulling towards her, its gaze fixed on her. As soon as the man and the dog got lost in the crowd, Mima broke into tears.

She was crying for her late husband. The feeling of loss hit her suddenly, unexpectedly. Her husband had come to see her in such a difficult moment for her, and they took him away by force, poor darling, they took him away on a leash and he couldn't give her a hug.

Mima kept weeping and sobbing on the bench, inconsolably. It was only now, more than a year after his physical death, that she realized how much she missed her husband.

Having cried her eyes out, Mima got up from the bench and headed home. There, Yehudi Menuhin was waiting for her – hungry, and longing for her. Her son was also waiting – hungry and longing. Mima had to take care of those two, instead of sitting on some bench, crying.

THE MAN WITH NO IDENTITY

Lyuba and Richard fell in love with each other when they were in college. Richard won Lyuba's heart with his maturity and completeness. They were only two years apart, but Lyuba had the feeling that she was getting hitched to an experienced man who could easily be her father. This gave her security and confidence.

Richard regarded women as weak creatures who needed protection and guidance. He summarized his condescending attitude with a single word – "Chicks!" – which he used with good-natured irony. Lyuba would get irritated by his patronizing tone, but with time, she came to realize that every man had his own way of loving women.

The couple's younger years passed like a dream. Lyuba gave Richard a son, not a daughter, and he was very happy. She won a competition for the post of assistant professor at the University, while he entered the top State administration as an expert, not as a party appointee, which meant he was a fixture there.

Richard's mother had named him after Richard the Lionheart. Lyuba liked her husband's name, which was highly unusual for Bulgaria, but when their newborn son was also registered as Richard, the name somehow lost its allure. Her son's birth certificate now read Richard Richardson Markov.

Lyuba and Richard were happy in their youth. Richard was a sociable and cheerful man. The couple had a lot of acquaintances and a bunch of close friends, with whom they often got together, partied, raised their kids, and climbed up the career ladder. The relationship between the two spouses fell into a certain order. Richard wore the pants in the house, while Lyuba pretended to obey him but in fact she did her own thing. He often criticized her, but she took his criticism with a smile and just winked at her friends. *"Nobody's perfect,"* that wink seemed to say.

Things began to change when young Richie got a bit older and his father took over his upbringing. He sent him to a daycare for diplomats' kids. At home, he spoke to him only in English. Richie's birthday parties resembled those in American movies: balloons, birthday hats, strap-on funny noses, confetti, speeches, the works.

Richard was not a mere cultural appropriator, but a senior civil servant with a vision. He dreamed of modernizing Bulgaria and did everything in his power. He despised the old order, laziness, irresponsibility, incompetence, party nominations. Sometimes he got in trouble and pestered Lyuba with his problems for days. He was outraged, he was suffering, and at such moments Lyuba liked him the most.

What Richard couldn't do for the State, he did for his son: he prepared him for the modern age. Young Richie was a dead ringer for his papa. Both of them were blond, blue-eyed and ruddy-cheeked. Richie had his father's posture, his gait, his manner of speaking: he was like a clone. Lyuba knew that Richard was trying to provide the best for their son, but his efforts were somewhat exaggerated. When a person gets obsessed with something, they reveal their true colors.

In the meantime, while listening in on the parental lectures and educational approaches Richard was using to raise his son, Lyuba found out that Richard had no thoughts of his own, or if he did, he did not share them with young Richie. He spoke such trite banalities, with such aplomb, that just listening to him made

Lyuba feel uncomfortable. She assumed that this was Richard's deliberate approach of conveying to the kid universally known, verified truths, but then she realized that Richard had no other approach. He repeated other people's banal thoughts, as if he had suffered through them.

Lyuba's observations about her husband piled up, one after the other. Richard not only copied other people's thoughts, he copied other people's intonations, too. At one point, he picked up this hyena laugh, exactly the way an acquaintance of theirs laughed. At other times, when overjoyed, he'd pound his fist on the table. He had borrowed this from a former college mate of his. Even "Chicks!", which was considered his trademark, turned out to be the trademark of one of his distant relatives – an uncouth hick.

Richard filled Ritchie's head with all sorts of nonsense, and Lyuba began to listen closely to their "man" talk. She'd step up to the threshold of her son's bedroom, her arms folded, forcing a faint smile that was meant to pass for housework fatigue, and would try to express a mixture of maternal and wife empathy. Lyuba was considering the idea of taking part in these conversations, but young Richie was no help to her at all. He was listening to his father enthralled, absorbing his words as if he was a prophet, and Lyuba hung back foolishly on the threshold like a redundant intruder.

With time, Richard took himself so seriously that his lectures extended to his wife, too. He scolded and instructed her, grumbled at her, and if before she had only smiled and winked at her friends, now she would blush and look down, burning with embarrassment.

She was also ashamed to hear Richard speak in the company of men: his voice rose and thundered, while the things he was saying were banal and silly, and Lyuba felt like plugging her ears. One evening, when he told her off in front of their guests, Lyuba blushed, then shouted, "Stop it!" and ran to the kitchen.

Her intolerance of Richard extended to his suits, colognes, the way he ate, the way he smiled and talked, the way he walked. She could not accept the fact that she had married a man who had no face of his own, no thoughts, not even words: like a parrot, he was repeating the words of the others. Richard was an empty space, hot air, and sometimes that scared her. She was shocked by the thought that she had respected an empty space. She wondered how she had fallen in love with Richard in the first place. He was mature and complete, yes, a mature and complete fool.

After meeting another man and becoming his mistress, Lyuba decided to leave her husband. Richard took the news badly. Even worse, he broke down. Lyuba felt sorry for him and put an end to her affair. The two tried to establish a new relationship with each other. Richard stopped putting on airs. He still talked nonsense, but no longer with such aplomb. His activities with Richie became more normal: he gave up his constant lecturing. Lyuba returned to her husband because of young Richie, and she even managed to salvage some of her devotion to the family.

The moment he sensed this, Richard gave himself airs again: his voice regained its assurance, and he began to reprimand her again. One night, he lost his temper and said, "I don't take advice from a woman who sleeps around!" At that very moment, Lyuba realized that she hated this man and they could not stay together a minute longer.

Their actual split-up went smoothly. Richard had realized that he wouldn't forgive Lyuba her infidelity, and it was best for both of them to part. Young Richie stayed with his father after his mother's official consent in court. Lyuba went to see him on pre-scheduled visitation days.

His parents' separation did not inflict trauma on young Richie. His father got him into a private high school with intensive English learning and set out to paving young Richie's way to a future career as a diplomat. The family relations among the three settled down.

One day, when Richie was fifteen, Lyuba was drinking coffee with a university colleague of hers. Her colleague was newly appointed and Lyuba was introducing her to the work they had to do together. The pastry shop in which the two women sat had large windows and was located in the city center.

At one point, Lyuba's colleague pointed to the street:

"Look at those two!... Father and son! See how funny they are!"

Lyuba turned her head and saw Richard and Richie on the opposite sidewalk.

The two walked side by side with the same gait, dressed in identical blue suits, with identical red ties, their blond hair combed in the same way. This sameness was so striking that passers-by turned to stare at them as if they were circus bears.

"Are they shooting a movie?" suggested Lyuba's colleague.

Richard and Richie were walking full of themselves, inaccessible, and apparently unaware of being the object of attention. A boy on the street followed them, imitating their gait, and passers-by stopped to stare and laugh.

Lyuba's colleague burst into laughter, too.

"Look how self-important they are! The pompous fools!"

Lyuba choked up. She excused herself and went to the ladies' room.

That was her son over there! And the father of her son! People were making fun of them, and she couldn't protect them.

Lyuba splashed tap water on her face and began to cry. The humiliation she had just experienced focused her entire life on the single moment when her son was walking next to his father, conceited, ridiculous, vulnerable, as naked as can be, and she was watching people make fun of him and couldn't help him. Her whole life wasn't worth a dime if she was unable to protect her child at a moment like this. Instead of fighting for him, she had left him in the hands of his father, who had turned him into the spitting image of himself.

Lyuba cried out loud. Her eyes swelled up. Tears streamed down her face and dripped on the tiles as if from a leaking tap.

AT THE OTHER END OF TOWN

Granny Tinka waited for her daughter to leave for work and set off to visit her grandson Georgi who was in prison. Granny Tinka had no idea what Georgi's crime was, her daughter wouldn't talk about him at all.

"I have no son any more!" she often said.

Tinka's granddaughter was blossoming into a woman, and she kept bugging her mother for pocket money. Granny Tinka's son-in-law had left her daughter, and the household struggled to make ends meet. Granny Tinka paid the utility bills with the remainder of her pension, and she was going to visit Georgi empty-handed. She didn't know how to find the prison, nor could she hear or see well. She had cataracts on both eyes. The operation to remove the cataracts was supposedly free for retirees, but it wasn't entirely so, so Granny Tinka had to endure and wait for things to get better. She'd probably never live to see things get better, but that didn't bother her. What really tormented Granny Tinka was whether she'd be able to see her grandson ever again before she died.

These days, Granny Tinka would only leave the house to buy bread. Her daughter had forbidden her to do other shopping as Tinka couldn't see how much money she was giving. At home, Granny Tinka tried to be useful, and she did the cooking every day. Once she seasoned a chicken stew with sugar instead of salt, and her daughter's shouts were heard around the neighborhood. After the chicken incident, Granny Tinka stopped cooking for fear of making another blunder. She stayed at home all day, wondering how to kill time.

Georgi was doing time in the Central Prison. Granny Tinka hadn't been there and didn't know where it was. She only knew it was at the other end of town. If her daughter knew what she was planning, there would be shouting, so Granny Tinka set off for the prison while her daughter was at work. She went out, passed by the store where she bought the bread and immediately lost her way. Trees and monotonous grey buildings blurred before her eyes. Only then did she appreciate the difficulty of her mission. She was so close to home, yet she didn't know how to return.

Someone walked past her. It turned out to be a woman.

"How do I get to the Central Prison," Granny Tinka asked.

"The Central Prison is all the way across town, dear. Let me think. Can you walk at all?"

Granny Tinka was blind and deaf, but she wasn't crippled. She had energy in excess, she just didn't know how to spend it. The kind lady led the way, and Granny Tinka followed her briskly. Soon, they reached a bus stop.

"Take this bus and ask the driver to let you off in the Ovcha Kupel neighborhood," the kind lady said. "When you get to Ovcha Kupel, ask someone where to go next."

Many years ago, Tinka and her late husband used to travel to their native village by taking a bus from the Ovcha Kupel bus station. This reassured Granny Tinka that she'd be able to find the way to the Central Prison.

In Ovcha Kupel, a boy told her to cross the boulevard and get the number 5 tram to the Russian Monument. Granny Tinka hoped the boy would take her to the tram stop, but he was going the other way, so she had to cross on her own. She heard horns and saw cars stopping right up to her.

Crossing the big boulevard had a refreshing effect on her. Granny Tinka felt as if she had outsmarted the entire traffic. When she reached the opposite sidewalk, she asked a man where the tram stop was. He said she shouldn't have crossed this boulevard, but the other one. He instructed her to go back and cross the other boulevard at the pedestrian crossing marked for that purpose.

Granny Tinka headed back, disregarding the cars. They let her pass once again, and she had the pleasant feeling she could do whatever she liked. Everyone treated her with consideration, and that had not happened for ages, if ever.

She reached the Russian Monument successfully. Once there, however, she took the 1 trolley in the wrong direction. After conquering Ovcha Kupel, Granny Tinka grew overconfident and forgot to ask in which direction to take the trolley bus. She asked three stops later and got off in some dark tunnel. The trolley bus departed, leaving her all alone. Cars were rushing by. She could make out their lights but couldn't see what was on the opposite side of the road where her stop was supposed to be.

At some point, Granny Tinka sensed a presence nearby and said:

"Excuse me, I'm lost. Where is the trolley bus stop in the opposite direction? I am blind, I can't see it, can you take me there, please?"

"Take you where?" a man's voice said in the dark.

"To the stop across the road."

"There's no stop across the road, grandma, there's only a concrete wall. The stop in the other direction is not here. Wait for the next trolley and ask someone to show you the way out of the underpass."

Out of all this, Granny Tinka gathered only that she should wait for the next trolley. To confirm, she asked:

"I'll wait for the next trolley bus?"

"Yes."

"And I get on?"

"No, don't get on. Ask someone to take you out of this underpass and show you the stop in the opposite direction."

"Okay, thank you."

When she was led out of the underpass, Granny Tinka found herself in some sort of a park. The woman who had assisted her pointed the direction and told her to go straight ahead until she reached Patriarch Evtimii Street, and once there, to ask where the number 1 trolley bus stop was.

To be on the safe side, Granny Tinka started asking everyone about the 1 trolley stop. Everyone told her to go straight ahead, and so she did, but then she'd ask again, lest she repeat her recent mistake, which was entirely due to her overconfidence. *"The road is rocky for the cocky,"* she thought to herself, remembering a childhood rhyme.

As soon as she got on the next trolley bus, she asked the driver if he was headed toward the Central Prison, but he said he was on a different route.

"This is the number 2, grandma, you need number 1. Get off and wait for it."

Granny Tinka got so startled that she jumped out of the trolley bus like a young lass.

Three hours after starting on her journey, she finally reached the last stop of the 1 trolley. She got off with the rest of the passengers, asked for directions to the prison and tried to follow them, but she immediately got lost in the back streets of the neighborhood. She started asking passers-by for help. Everyone told her the prison was very close: take the first right, then left, and it's right there. She took the first right, walked and walked, but the prison wasn't there. So she asked again.

The prison was still very close: take the first left, go straight, can't miss it.

Granny Tinka started to panic. The streets were quiet and deserted, the sun was shining, birds were singing. *"So close, yet so far,"* she thought. Every now and then she stopped to peer in the distance, hoping to see something resembling a prison building. At one point, she decided not to ask anymore, but to keep on walking and hope for the best. She dared not think about her trip back home.

Despite her energy and stamina, Granny Tinka eventually got tired and stopped for a breather under the shade of a tree. Was this how her journey was going to end? In the middle of nowhere? But if this was indeed rock bottom, things could only get better, right?

Refreshed by these questions, Granny Tinka continued onwards.

Soon, she reached a large street with a lot of traffic, and asked a man for directions.

"The prison? This is it."

"Where?"

"Right in front of you."

Right in front of her, there was only a high wall which she had seen a few times already.

"Is this the prison?" she asked in disbelief.

"Yes. Cross the street, follow the wall on your left and you'll reach the central entrance."

Granny Tinka literally ran across the street. She heard a car honk behind her back, but paid it no mind, and once she reached the opposite sidewalk, she scurried toward the entrance.

Clasping her ID card, she explained to security that she wanted to pay a visit to her grandson. She was told that visiting hours were during the weekend.

"I can't come during the weekend," she said.

"You can only visit on Saturday and Sunday, grandma."

Granny Tinka had anticipated this bad outcome, but she had no choice. Her daughter was always at home during the weekend. Granny Tinka had hoped that the prison security would show mercy and let her visit her grandson, but that didn't happen, so she decided to stand by the entrance and wait, hoping to see Georgi by chance. She'd heard that some prisoners have day jobs in the city, and she imagined Georgi leaving for work and seeing her there, by the gate. She hoped she could see him, too, but that was not that important. What mattered was for Georgi to see her and know that his family hadn't given up on him.

Granny Tinka stood guard by the gate until her legs gave up. On the other side of the gate there was a small building with people coming and going. Granny Tinka entered through the glass door. She smelled coffee. The small café had several tables, and she sat down at the one closest to the door, so that she could return to her post in case something should happen.

Two hours passed. At some point, a woman approached Granny Tinka.

"Waiting for someone, dear?"

"My grandson's inside, I want to see him."

"What's his job?"

"He's a prisoner."

"Did you ask at the gate?"

"Yes."

"Didn't they tell you there's no visits today?"

"They did."

The woman considered this and walked away. In a moment, she came back and set in front of Granny Tinka a sweet bun and a plastic cup.

"Do you drink coffee?"

"Don't mind if I do."

"Drink this and have a bite, I brought you a bun, it's fresh."

"Such a kind woman," Granny Tinka thought. *"There are good people everywhere!"*

While she was eating the soft bun, she kept an eye on the prison gate, but apart from the uniformed men coming and going, nothing much was happening there. After she ate the bun, Granny Tinka felt sleepy. She dozed off, then suddenly the kind woman and a uniformed man appeared right in front of her. The man asked her something and waited for an answer, but Granny Tinka had slept through his question.

"I can't hear very well," she said.

"What's your grandson's name?"

"Georgi. Georgi Parvanov."

The man laughed, "Same as the President?"

"Same as the President," Granny Tinka said.

"What is he in for?"

"I don't know, I wasn't told."

"There's no visits today, grandma. Come again on Saturday or Sunday."

"I can't. It's not possible."

"Does your grandson have any other relatives?"

"Yes."

"Parents?"

"Yes, but they are divorced."

"Have them visit him instead."

"They won't come."

"Why not?"

Granny Tinka didn't reply.

"You'll have to come back during the weekend, grandma, no visits today."

Granny Tinka thought for a moment and said:

"Will you give my grandson a message?"

The uniformed man laughed:

"Sure. What is it?"

"Tell him his grandma was here. Tell him we think of him at home. And we hope he returns soon. And tell him to be good."

Granny Tinka wanted to say much more, but she suddenly ran out of words and fell silent.

"Georgi Parvanov, right?" the uniformed man asked.

"Georgi Parvanov, same as the President."

"I'll give him your message, grandma. Go home now, I'll let him know you were here. And tell his mother to come visit him."

"Thank you! Thank you so much!" Granny Tinka said and stood up from the chair.

The uniformed man saw her to the gate and headed back to the café. Suddenly, Granny Tinka called after him:

"I'm his Granny Tinka, on his mother's side. He has another grandmother, too. Tell him Granny Tinka was here, on his mother's side!"

"Alright, got it, don't worry, I'll tell him."

"On his mother's side, not on his father's."

After this conversation, Granny Tinka left confidently, as if she knew the way back home. Her heart was light and joyful. She marched along the back streets the way she had marched in Labor Day parades back in her youth. Back then, the people would go out on parades, and afterwards there was food and drinks and dancing. She and her husband were laborers from the countryside. They spent their lives at the Voroshilov plant. Her husband died young, he didn't make it to retirement. During the parades, they'd sing laborer marching songs that filled her with joy. Her favorite march was *Working Men and Women, Unite!*

Walking among the little old houses of her youth, Granny Tinka was humming that march and stepping to its beat. She

     LUDMIL TODOROV

wasn't thinking about the direction. She wasn't thinking whether she'd find her way. Her life at home was like her grandson's life in prison. Now that she had done her duty of letting him know his folks hadn't forgotten him, she did not intend to take into consideration anything else at all: not her blindness, nor her daughter, let alone the public transport.

Soon, Granny Tinka reached a big boulevard. Cars were rushing by at 100 kilometers per hour. While she was listening to their noise, Granny Tinka felt the insurmountable urge to do some sort of mischief.

As a child, she'd often been tempted to break the hens' eggs in the chicken coop. Once she broke them all without knowing why. Now she was tempted to cross the boulevard and watch the drivers struggle with the difficult task of sparing her.

The buzzing cars came in waves along the boulevard like swarms of vicious wasps. Granny Tinka waited for the next wave to approach and stepped down onto the street.

HOW WONDERFUL!

That spring Mima stared at the sky as if she had never seen it before. People notice the sky when it is purple or orange, when it's overcast with heavy rain clouds, or when it has that blue color that makes you want to fly. Mima would stare at the sky even when there was nothing to stare at, and that's exactly what the sky over Sofia is usually like – gray, low, and dull.

"How wonderful!" she would exclaim, taking a picture of it.

People seldom think of looking up at the sky. What they usually do is complain about it. The only critters that never complain about anything are the sheep, and Mima had a soft spot for them. Sheep are patient, quiet and beautiful. Yes, beautiful. Mima called them "baby-dolls". When she happened to travel outside the city, she always took pictures of sheep with her phone.

Mima's cat, Yehudi Menuhin, died in the winter. Yehudi was born in a village under the name of Kicko. After opening her home up to him, Mima named him after her favorite violin-player.

Yehudi turned out to be a fine aristoc(r)at. He didn't much care for food or attention. He was a born contemplator. He observed life peering from around a corner. He was a delicate, sensitive feline, and losing him hit Mima hard.

Yehudi had white, silky fur and shedded like a sheep. Each time Mima combed his hair (God, how he hated that!) she collected his fluff in a plastic bag. Her son once asked her why she was collecting Yehudi's hair and she jokingly replied she was going to knit a sweater. Her son, young enough to believe her at the time, was delighted to hear that and, from then on, started calling Yehudi "little sheep."

After Yehudi's death, life invaded Mima with unprecedented force. She saw through appearances with ease. For instance, when she watched a stray dog run with a busy and purposeful air, she somehow knew that the dog didn't have the slightest idea where it was headed. Nothing cheered her up more than the chirping of a sparrow intent on showing the whole world how stupid it is. Riding the bus to work, she'd read the petty thoughts of a vain retiree and smile amiably at him, which would totally puzzle him.

All living creatures – people and animals alike – appeared to share the same lust for life. That filled Mima with both joy and anguish. Due to that universal lust she sometimes felt like crying: everybody seemed so lost, helpless, and dear to her. It was only her beloved Yehudi who didn't lust after anything, and Mima was proud to have lived with such a great and noble cat.

There were mornings when Mima saw the world as if for the first time. A broad smile would appear on her face, not leaving it all day. Everything felt so precious and intimate. And she kept uttering these two words:

"How wonderful!"

She'd start her day with a few pictures of the sky. The photo shoot continued on the street, where Mima would stop in front of a poplar tree and photograph it, imagining it was budding and would be leafing any moment now. Then she showed the pictures to her acquaintances and asked them if they could see the green blood running through the poplar twigs' veins. No one saw anything, as the green blood was only running in Mima's head.

On the way to the bus stop, she walked past a mean dog, which barked and rushed at her to bite her.

The dog lived in an open yard, unleashed, and never let her pass without growling and lunging at her. Mima would freeze in her tracks, the dog barking at her from two steps away, and she'd say in a cautionary voice:

"C'mon, boy, don't be ridiculous!"

The dog got into a frenzy of barking, baring its teeth.

Mima waited till the dog got tired and walked on, her heart pounding madly. That was the moment she'd say to herself:

"How wonderful!"

It was wonderful that the dog didn't bite her – that's what she meant.

Her husband, who had passed away quite young, often used to recall a road-trip to the countryside that the two of them had taken once.

It was a bitterly cold winter. They were driving down a country road, when a small frozen pond appeared in the middle of the snow field by the road, and Mima said:

"How wonderful that we're not there, ice-skating!"

Neither she nor her husband skated. What's more, neither of them liked any sports. How Mima had seen herself skating in that deserted, unfriendly place, was a mystery only her husband could explain. How wonderful to be in the warm car, and not out in the cold: this is how Mima thanked fate for being good to her.

People like complaining about fate, and sometimes Mima felt like the head of a Complaints bureau. She had three kinds of "clients". The first ones complained with a smile. Listening to them made Mima sad.

The second ones took a long time to complain. Mima listened absently to them as she knew they just wanted to make a little fuss over themselves.

The third ones were the hardest. This type of people wanted to prove by all means that their lives were unbearable. When Mima tried to calm them down, questioning the weight of their burden, they got offended.

One day, a cousin of hers got so worked up pouring out her complaints, that she ended up crying out loud. In an attempt to cheer her up, Mima showed her some pictures of sheep.

"See how patient and beautiful they are!" she said.

Her cousin took the sheep photos as an incredible insult and left in a huff.

Mima predisposed people towards confession, without doing anything special. Few of her acquaintances realized she knew everything about them, while they knew barely anything about her. After each session, Mima would get a splitting headache and wonder how to get rid of the thoughts crammed into her head by the others. She looked up at the sky and stared at it for a long time. A small crevice between the gray clouds was enough for her to get a sense of the infinite, the beyond.

Fate had first deprived her of a husband, and now – of her beloved cat; Mima needed to gaze at the sky, photograph it, admire the pictures for a good couple of hours, and, in the meantime, let her soul soar.

After each confession, Mima would come home totally beat. She seemed like someone carrying a glass full of water, careful not to splash it. She felt as if her head was clenched in a vise. At such moments, she was numb with pain, drained of all strength. Her whole body stiffened. She couldn't sleep, she couldn't do anything. She took strong painkillers.

In the wee hours of the night, the pills would take effect, the pain would subside, and just before falling asleep, Mima would whisper, quietly:

"How wonderful!"

ABOUT THE TEAM

LUDMIL TODOROV, author: Ludmil Todorov is a contemporary Bulgarian writer and film director. He is the author of three collections of short stories and five novels. He has written and directed six feature films, highly appraised at national and international film festivals. Both his films and his books vividly portray the life and the people of present-day Bulgaria. He is married and lives in Sofia.

ZLATNA KOSTOVA, translator: Zlatna Kostova is a Bulgarian translator, journalist and the author of two poetry books. She translates plays for the stage, movies, TV programs and books, among which is *To Thee I Sing* by Barack Obama. Her translations of American and British playwrights have been produced at every theater in Sofia and throughout Bulgaria. Chekhov's first play *Ivanov*, which she translated from the Russian, is still played at Sofia's Youth Theater. She is married and lives in Sofia.

MATEY TODOROV, translator: Matey Todorov translates poetry, prose, films, TV series, librettos for musicals and plays for the stage from and into English. He translated many plays by American and English playwrights, which are now playing at major Bulgarian theaters, among them those of Woody Allen and Sarah Ruhl. He lives in Sofia and works at the Bulgaria News Agency.

BISSERA KOSTOVA, editor: Bissera Kostova was born in Bulgaria and split her childhood years between Sofia and New York. She has spent most of her career working in communications at the United Nations and is currently managing the UN website. She is married and lives in Brooklyn.